100 SKETCHES OF HUMAN BEHAVIOUR FROM GREAT NOVELS

外國名著行為描寫一百段

一百叢書⑳

英漢對照English-Chinese

郭麗 選譯　張信威 主編

外國名著
行爲描寫一百段
100
SKETCHES OF
HUMAN
BEHAVIOUR
FROM
GREAT NOVELS

臺灣商務印書館發行

《一百叢書》總序

本館出版英漢（或漢英）對照《一百叢書》的目的，是希望憑藉着英、漢兩種語言的對譯，把中國和世界各類著名作品的精華部分介紹給中外讀者。

本叢書的涉及面很廣。題材包括了寓言、詩歌、散文、短篇小説、書信、演説、語錄、神話故事、聖經故事、成語故事、名著選段等等。

顧名思義，《一百叢書》中的每一種都由一百個單元組成。以一百為單位，主要是讓編譯者在浩瀚的名著的海洋中作挑選時有一個取捨的最低和最高限額。至於取捨的標準，則是見仁見智，各有心得。

由於各種書中被選用的篇章節段，都是以原文或已被認定的範本作藍本，而譯文又經專家學者們精雕細琢，千錘百煉，故本叢書除可作為各種題材的精選讀本外，也是研習英漢兩種語言對譯的理想參考書，部分更可用作朗誦教材。外國學者如要研習漢語，本書亦不失為理想工具。

商務印書館 (香港) 有限公司

編輯部

前　言

　　行為是人們思想和個性的表現。行為描寫是文學作品
中刻劃人物的重要手法。而富有典型意義的行為描寫可以
使人物的形象更加生動，給讀者留下深刻的印象。

　　行為往往是由一連串動作構成的。名家在行為描寫時
尤善於捕捉人物特別的動作，配上恰當的詞彙及意象，從
而準確地表現了人物的性格特徵，使人物形象活靈活現。
狄更斯在《遠大前程》中描寫匹普的姐姐切麵包的動作
時，在短短的幾行文字中，就用了三個表示 "切" 的動詞：
"cut our bread-and-butter"、"sawed a very thick round off
the loaf"、"hewed it into halves"。"cut" 是個最常見的詞，
"saw" 是形容她切下一片麵包時拉鋸似的動作，"hew" 是指
將麵包一切兩半時砍柴似的動作。幾個動詞都用得貼切、
具體及形象化，描寫細緻入微。這同時也顯示了作家對生
活細節的細緻觀察和駕馭語言的才能。

　　行為描寫不僅包含人物在重大矛盾衝突中的行為，也
常涉及人物在日常生活中的行為，如：進餐、就寢、唱
歌、跳舞等。在重大矛盾衝突中，人的行動最能反映其內
心世界與個性。《牛虻》中有這樣一段情節：篤信天主教
的阿瑟，發現自己受到了宗教的愚弄和欺騙，於是他憤然
揮起鎚子，砸碎了神像。這時的牛虻處於極大的感情矛盾
中，他的行動表現了他與宗教及神權決裂的決心。

本書選材的範圍主要是十八至二十世紀的歐美文學名
著，全書選用了四十二位作家的五十三部作品中的片段。
作家大部分為英美兩國的，也有法國、俄國、德國的。

人的行為千姿百態，本書所選的只是滄海一粟。但這
裏包含了日常生活中最常見的一些行動，可大致分為以下
各類：

—— 動作類：起床、更衣、洗澡、跳舞、游水、打架
　　等；
—— 生理類：饑餓、疲倦、疾病、生育、死亡等；
—— 感情、心理類：哭、笑、痛苦、絕望、恐懼、驚慌
　　等；
—— 婚戀家庭類：親吻、擁抱、求婚、蜜月、分離等；
—— 勞作類：播種、打獵等；
—— 社群活動類：晚會、聚餐、競選等；
—— 宗教、司法類：布道、裁決等；
—— 風俗類：送殯、占卜等；
—— 戰爭類：受傷、搶救等。

為避免與其他《一百叢書》的主題重複，心理與愛情
方面的題材未過多選入，只選擇了部分動作性很強的篇
目。另外，一些消極及罪惡的行為，如：賭博、盜竊、搶
劫、殺人等，都不選入。由於篇幅所限，對與動作或主題

無關的部分原文作了少量刪節，而刪去的句子或段落以省略號代替。

　　考慮到本書的讀者應有一定的英文水平，注釋方面側重對原文的賞析，如選篇的寫作特點、對情節內容的提示、人物的簡要介紹、原文提及的名人典故、以及有關文化背景方面的知識。語言上的注解則注重一些難度較高或較生僻的詞在選文中的具體涵意或引申意義，古詞今用，以及部分修辭手法。有許多字詞看起來雖然較難，但在一般字典中有明確的解釋，這種情況一般未加注釋。

　　此書從選材、翻譯、到加注，基本由本選譯者獨立完成。譚載喜教授仔細閱覽了全部譯文和注解，作了許多修改，加入了一些關於寫作特點、翻譯手法等方面的注解，並提出了許多寶貴的意見及指導，使本書得以順利完成。在編譯過程中，編者也參考了少量已出版的譯著，特此說明。

　　希望讀者能藉此書欣賞到文學名家對人類行為的精彩描寫，並能增強英語語言知識，提高英文寫作水平。

　　錯漏之處在所難免，敬請各位專家與讀者不吝指教。

郭麗

一九九六年七月

Preface

Man's behaviour reveals his thoughts and personality. In literary works the description of behaviour is an important means to portray characters and typical description of specific behaviour can render the image of a character more vivid and memorable.

Human behaviour usually consists of a series of acts . A master in literature is capable of capturing the characteristic acts of his characters and applying proper vocabulary and imagery so as to create a lively and lifelike description. In *Great Expectations*, for example, Dickens uses three different verbs to depict how Pip's sister cut the bread : "cut our bread-and-butter", "sawed a very thick round off the loaf", "hewed it into halves". The depiction begins with "cut", a very ordinary word, while "hew" denotes cutting by striking blows, as with an ax or a weapon, and "saw" suggests moving one's hands forward and backwards as if cutting with a saw. Each verb is accurately and vividly used, making the description detailed and impressive. This fully demonstrates the writer's meticulous observation of life and his mastery and manipulation of his language.

The description of behaviour involves the behaviour of a character not only in major conflicts but also in everyday life, for instance, eating, sleeping, singing and dancing. In a major emotional conflict, a man's behaviour best reflects his inner self and personality. In *The Gadfly*, when Arthur who had been a devout believer in Catholicism found that he was fooled by the religion, he smashed the crucifix with a hammer. In his emotional fit, he showed his determination to break with the religion and God.

The 100 excerpts in this book are taken from 53 novels or short stories written in the 18th - 20th century by 42 authors — mostly from Great Britain and the United States and some from France, Russia and Germany.

The human behaviour depicted in this book falls roughly into the following categories:

— physical action: getting up, dancing, swimming, fighting, etc.;
— behaviour with a physiological origin: feeling hungry or tired, falling ill, dying, etc.;
— emotion-driven behaviour: crying, laughing, and behaviour in despair, fear or panic, etc.;
— behaviour involving romantic love and the family: kissing, embracing, making a marriage proposal, enjoying a honeymoon, etc.;
— labour: sowing, hunting, etc.;
— social activities: having dinner parties, running elections, etc.;
— religion and law: preaching, court trials, etc.;

— social customs: attending a funeral, telling fortune, etc.;

— war: getting wounded, rescue.

To avoid repeating the themes of the other books in *The One Hundred Series*, I have not selected too many passages concerning emotion, psychology and love. But some overlapping is inevitable and such pieces are chosen because they are full of action. Some negative and even criminal behaviour, for example, gambling, theft, robbery, murder, is not included. Because of limited space, certain sentences or paragraphs which are not relevant to the theme are left out and replaced by ellipsis.

Assuming that the readers of this book have a sufficient knowledge of English, the annotations are there only to facilitate the appreciation of the excerpts: they focus on the style and characteristics of writing, cues on the plots, brief information about the characters and famous personages, allusions and cultural background. Explanations on language points concern mainly difficult or uncommon words with their specific or extended meanings in the selections, ancient words in modern use and some figures of speech.

Special thanks should be given to Professor Tan Zaixi who carefully read through all the Chinese translations and notes, made changes and added some explanations on writing and translation techniques. His valuable suggestions and guidance had facilitated my translation work, in the process of which I had also consulted a few translated works.

I hope the readers can enjoy the brilliant descriptions of human behaviour in this book and, at the same time, enrich their knowledge in the English language and improve their writing ability.

Guo Li
July, 1996

目　錄
CONTENTS

1 Getting up

RRRRRRRRIIIIIIIIIIIIIIIIIIIINNG!

An alarm clock clanged in the dark and silent room. A bed spring creaked. A woman's voice sang out impatiently:

"Bigger, shut that thing off!"

A surly grunt sounded above the tinny ring of metal. Naked feet swished dryly[1] across the planks in the wooden floor and the clang ceased abruptly.

"Turn on the light, Bigger."

"Awright," came a sleepy mumble.

Light flooded the room and revealed a black boy standing in a narrow space between two iron beds, rubbing his eyes with the backs of his hands. From a bed to his right the woman spoke again:

"Buddy, get up from there! I got a big washing on my hands today and I want you all out of here."

Another black boy rolled from bed and stood up. The woman also rose and stood in her nightgown.

---

1. swished dryly：沙沙作響；這裏指光着腳在木板地上走動時乾爽的聲音。

一　起牀

叮鈴鈴鈴鈴鈴鈴鈴鈴！

鬧鐘在安靜而又黑暗的房間裏響了起來。牀墊咯吱咯吱一陣響。一個女人不耐煩的喊道：

"比格，把那玩意關了！"

一陣沒好氣的咕噥聲蓋過了鬧鐘的叮鈴聲。光着的腳丫子啪噠啪噠踩着木頭地板走過來，鬧鐘立刻不響了。

"開燈，比格。"

"嗯，"傳來帶着睡意的咕噥聲。

燈光照亮了房間，可以看到一個黑孩子站在兩張鐵牀中間的狹窄空間裏，用手背揉着眼睛。他右邊牀上的那個女人又說話了：

"布迪，起來！今天我有一大堆衣服要洗，我要你們統統出去。"

另一個黑孩子滚下牀，站起身。那個女人也起來了，穿着睡衣站在那裏。

"Turn your heads so I can dress," she said.

The two boys averted their eyes and gazed into a far corner of the room. The woman rushed out of her nightgown and put on a pair of step-ins[2]. She turned to the bed from which she had risen and called:

"Vera! Get up from there!"

"What time is it, Ma?" asked a muffled, adolescent voice from beneath a quilt.

"Get up from there, I say!"

"O.K., Ma."

A brown-skinned girl in a cotton gown got up and stretched her arms above her head and yawned. Sleepily, she sat on a chair and fumbled with her stockings. The two boys kept their faces averted while their mother and sister put on enough clothes to keep them from feeling ashamed; and the mother and sister did the same while the boys dressed.

Richard Wright: Native Son

---

2. step-ins：（先把腿伸入然後拉起穿上的）女式內衣。

“把頭轉過去，我好穿衣服。”

兩個男孩移開目光，盯着房間遠處的一個角落。那女人迅速脫下睡袍，換上內衣，然後轉向她剛睡的那張牀，嚷道：

“維拉，起牀。”

“幾點了，媽？”一個捂在被子裏的少女的聲音問。

“起來呀，我説！”

“好吧，媽。”

一個穿着棉布睡袍、棕色皮膚的女孩從牀上起身，兩臂伸展過頭頂，打着呵欠。她睡眼惺忪地坐在椅子上，摸索着穿上長統襪。兩個男孩一直背着臉，好讓媽媽和妹妹多穿些衣服，免得感到難為情；男孩子們穿衣服的時候，媽媽和妹妹也同樣背着臉。

　　　　　　　　　　(美) 理查·賴特：《土生子》

2 To Take Off Her Boots[1]

Ma Parker drew the two jetty spears out of her toque and hung it behind the door. She unhooked her worn jacket and hung that up too. Then she tied her apron and sat down to take off her boots. To take off her boots or to put them on was an agony to her, but it had been an agony for years. In fact, she was so accustomed to the pain that her face was drawn and screwed up ready for the twinge before she'd so much as untied the laces. That over, she sat back with a sigh and softly rubbed her knees....[2]

Katherine Mansfield: "Life Of Ma Parker"

---

1. 此段描述了一位貧窮的老太太在替人做家務前更衣的情景。雖然寥寥幾筆，但卻細緻生動。
2. 帕克大娘似有腿疾。

二 更衣

　　帕克大娘從帽子上摘下兩隻簪子，把帽子掛在門後。
再解開破舊的外套，也掛在門後。然後她繫上圍裙，坐下
來脫靴子。穿、脫靴子對她來説是件痛苦的事，多年來一
直如此。實際上，她對此已經十分習慣，甚至在沒有解開
鞋帶，痛苦尚未到來的時候，她的面部肌肉就緊張起來，
眉頭緊蹙。靴子脫下來了，她嘆息着坐下，輕輕地揉着膝
蓋……

　　　　　　（英）凱瑟琳·曼斯菲爾德：《帕克大娘的一生》

3 A Man Washing Himself [1]

In the little yard two paces beyond her, the man was washing himself, utterly unaware. He was naked to the hips, his velveteen breeches slipping down over his slender loins. And his white slim back was curved over a big bowl of soapy water, in which he ducked his head, shaking his head with a queer, quick little motion, lifting his slender white arms, and pressing the soapy water from his ears, quick, subtle as a weasel playing with water, and utterly alone. Connie backed away from the corner of the house and hurried away to the wood. In spite of herself[2], she had had a shock. After all, merely a man washing himself, commonplace enough, Heaven knows[3]!

D.H. Lawrence: Lady Chatterley's Lover

---

1. 查特萊夫人 (Connie) 去給守林人送口信，無意之中看到他在洗澡，她清楚地感到一陣震顫。
2. in spite of herself：不由自主。
3. Heaven knows：(用以加強語氣) 確實，無疑。這是 Connie 在試圖使自己冷靜下來。

三　洗澡

在小院裏，距她兩步遠的地方，那個男子正在洗澡，對她的到來毫無察覺。他的身體裸露至臀部，棉絨短褲滑落到他瘦削的腰下。白皙而細長的脊背彎曲着，下面放着一大盆肥皂水。他不時地把頭浸入水中，迅速而怪樣地甩動着腦袋，並舉起白而細瘦的雙臂，不停地壓迫着耳朵，讓裏面的肥皂水流出來。他的動作迅速而靈敏，儼然一隻鼬鼠獨自在嬉水。康尼順着牆角退回去，匆匆走進樹林，她不禁感到怦然心跳。只不過是個男人在洗澡，確實再尋常不過了！

（英）勞倫斯：《查特萊夫人的情人》

4　To Be in Bed[1]

His fingers trembled as he undressed himself in the dormitory. He told his fingers to hurry up. He had to undress and then kneel and say his own prayers and be in bed before the gas was lowered so that he might not go to hell when he died. He rolled his stockings off and put on his nightshirt quickly and knelt trembling at his bedside and repeated his prayers quickly, quickly, fearing that the gas would go down.

...

He blessed himself and climbed quickly into bed and, tucking the end of the nightshirt under his feet, curled himself together under the cold white sheets, shaking and trembling.

James Joyce: A Portrait of the Artist as a Young Man

1.　六歲的 Stephen 在一個天主教的寄宿學校上學。本選段是他在一個寒冷的夜晚上牀時的情景。

四 就寢

他在宿舍裏脫衣服的時候，冷得十指發抖。他命令自己的手指動作快一些。在暖氣關小之前，他得脫好衣服，跪下唸禱文，然後上牀，這樣他死後就不會下地獄了。他脫下襪子，迅速穿上睡袍，哆哆嗦嗦地跪在牀邊，以很快，很快的速度唸着禱文，害怕暖氣會冷下去。

……

他在胸前劃了個十字，很快地爬上牀，用睡袍的下擺裹住腳，蓋上冰涼的白被單，全身縮成一團，不停地哆嗦着。

(英) 喬伊斯：《藝術家年青時期的畫像》

5   Cutting Our Bread-and-Butter

My sister had a trenchant way of cutting our bread-and-butter for us, that never varied. First, with her left hand she jammed the loaf hard and fast against her bib — where it sometimes got a pin into it, and sometimes a needle[1], which we afterwards got into our mouths. Then she took some butter (not too much) on a knife and spread it on the loaf, in an apothecary kind of way, as if she were making a plaister[2] — using both sides of the knife with a slapping dexterity, and trimming and moulding the butter off round the crust. Then, she gave the knife a final smart wipe on the edge of the plaister, and then sawed a very thick round off the loaf: which she finally, before separating from the loaf, hewed[3] into two halves, of which Joe got one, and I the other.

Charles Dickens: <u>Great Expectations</u>

---

1. ＂我＂的姐姐天天帶着圍裙，上面總是別着很多針，以顯示自己的勤勞。
2. plaister： ＝ plaster

五 切麵包

　　我姐姐切麵包、抹黃油非常麻利，手法也是一成不變的。首先，她用左手把一長條麵包牢牢地頂在圍裙上部── 有時一隻大頭針或縫衣針便會扎到麵包上，隨後會進到我們的嘴裏。然後她用刀子切下一點黃油（不會太多），抹在長麵包上，那樣子像個藥劑師在做膏藥 ── 用刀子的兩面塗來抹去，快速而靈活，再把麵包皮上的黃油刮掉。最後她動作敏捷地把刀子在"膏藥"邊上一抹，從長麵包上切下厚厚的一圈，未切到底的時候，又一刀將它一分為二，一半給喬，一半給我。

(英) 狄更斯：《遠大前程》

---

3. hewed： 這一段用了三個表示"切"的動詞：cut 是最普通和常用的詞；saw 則強調切的時候有拉鋸似的動作；hewed 有"砍"、"劈"的涵義，猶如劈柴的動作。幾個詞都用得貼切而生動。

6 Eating[1]

There was a pause, while he noted with mild surprise how much and how quickly she was eating. The remains of a large pool of sauce were to be seen on her plate beside a diminishing mound of[2] fried egg, bacon, and tomatoes. Even as he watched she replenished her stock of sauce with a fat scarlet gout from the bottle. She glanced up and caught his look of interest, raised her eyebrows, and said, "I'm sorry, I like sauce; I hope you don't mind," but not convincingly, and he fancied she blushed.

"That's all right," he said heartily, "I'm fond of the stuff myself." He pushed aside his bowl of cornflakes. They were of a kind he didn't like; malt had been used in their preparation. A study of the egg and bacon and tomatoes opposite him made him decide to postpone eating any himself. His gullet and stomach felt as if they were being deftly sewed up as he sat. He poured a cup of black coffee, then refilled his cup.

Kingsley Amis: Lucky Jim

---

1. 此篇描述兩人共進早餐的情景,一個是狼吞虎嚥,另一個則是毫無胃口。作者對進食與不進食的動作作了細膩描寫,使其形成對照。

2. a diminishing mound of:一大堆逐漸減少的⋯⋯。

14

六　共進早餐

　　兩人靜了下來，狄克遜觀察到她東西吃得那麼多，那麼快，心裏不免感到有幾分詫異。碟子上堆滿的雞蛋、腌肉和西紅柿已經掃去了一半，加在旁邊的一大攤調味汁也只剩下一些痕迹。即使是他在旁邊望着，她還是又拿起盛調味汁的瓶子，將紅色的醬汁又往盤子上倒了一大堆。隨後，她抬起頭，碰上狄克遜饒有興致的目光，蹙了蹙眉，說：“對不起，我很喜歡調味汁，你不介意吧。”但語氣不太令人信服，狄克遜彷彿覺得她的臉刷地變紅了。

　　“沒甚麼，”他誠懇地說，“這東西我也喜歡吃。”他把給他的一碗玉米片推開，這種玉米片裏加了麥芽，他不喜歡。望見對面桌上的雞蛋、腌肉和西紅柿，他這會兒一點東西也不想吃了。他坐在那兒，感到喉嚨和肚子被人靈巧地縫上了似的。他倒了一杯咖啡，沒攙牛奶，喝完後又倒一杯。

　　　　　　　　（英）金斯萊·艾米斯：《幸運的吉姆》

7 He Ate in a Ravenous Way

He ate in a ravenous way that was very disagreeable, and all his actions were uncouth, noisy and greedy. Some of his teeth had failed him since I saw him eat on the marshes, and as he turned his food in his mouth, and turned his head sideways to bring his strongest fangs to bear on it, he looked terribly like a hungry dog.

Charles Dickens: Great Expectations

七　狼吞虎嚥

　　他狼吞虎嚥，吃相很不雅觀，一舉一動都是那麼粗魯
和貪婪，嚼東西時發出很大的聲響。當年我曾見過他在沼
澤地裏的吃相，與那時相比，他少了幾顆牙齒。只見他嘴
裏翻來覆去嚼個不停，同時側着腦袋，好用那幾顆最硬的
尖牙去啃，樣子活像一條餓荒的老狗。

（英）狄更斯：《遠大前程》

8 Scanned the Bill of Fare

They found a place that looked quite cheap. But when
Mrs Morel scanned the bill of fare, her heart was heavy, things
were so dear. So she ordered kidney pies and potatoes as the
cheapest available dish.

"We oughtn't to have come here, mother," said Paul.

"Never mind," she said. "We won't come again."

She insisted on his having a small currant tart, because
he liked sweets.

"I don't want it, mother," he pleaded.

"Yes," she insisted, "you'll have it."

And she looked round for the waitress. But the waitress
was busy, and Mrs Morel did not like to bother her then. So
the mother and son waited for the girl's pleasure, whilst she
flirted among the men.

"Brazen hussy!" said Mrs Morel to Paul. "Look now,
she's taking that man his pudding, and he came long after
us."

"It doesn't matter, mother," said Paul.

Mrs Morel was angry. But she was too poor, and her

八　點菜

　　他們找了一個看似便宜的飯館。但是莫雷爾太太掃了一眼價目表，心情變得沉重起來，東西太貴了。她點了一個最便宜的菜，腰子餡餅加馬鈴薯。

　　"我們不該來這裏，媽媽，"保羅説。

　　"沒關係，"她説，"下不為例。"

　　她執意給他點一個提子餡餅，因為他喜歡甜食。

　　"我不要，媽媽，"他懇求道。

　　"要的，"她很堅決，"你要吃。"

　　她環顧四周找女侍應，但女侍應正忙着，莫雷爾太太一時不想打攪她。於是母子二人便等待着，等她高興的時候來招呼他們，而她卻在男人中間打情罵俏。

　　"不要臉的賤人！"莫雷爾太太對保羅説，"你看，她在給那個男人上布丁，可他來得比我們晚得多。"

　　"沒關係的，媽媽，"保羅説。

　　莫雷爾太太生氣了。但是她太窮，點的東西微不足

orders were too meagre, so that she had not the courage to insist on her rights just then. They waited and waited[1].

"Should we go, mother?" he said.

Then Mrs Morel stood up. The girl was passing near.

"Will you bring one currant tart?" said Mrs Morel clearly. The girl looked round insolently.

"Directly," she said.

"We have waited quite long enough," said Mrs Morel.

In a moment the girl came back with the tart. Mrs Morel asked coldly for the bill. Paul wanted to sink through the floor. He marvelled at his mother's hardness. He knew that only years of battling had taught her to insist even so little on her rights. She shrank as much as he.

"It's the last time I go *there* for anything!"[2] she declared, when they were outside the place, thankful to be clear.

D.H. Lawrence: <u>Sons and Lovers</u>

---

1. waited and waited: 這類重複動詞的英語結構，相當於漢語的 "等了又等"，兩者的結構意義十分相似。

2. 此句中 there 一詞用斜體，具有強調的意思。漢語中不宜用變換字體來表示這層意思，而往往需要根據上下文做增詞處理。

道，所以一時沒有勇氣堅持自己的權利。他們又等了很久。

"媽媽，我們是不是該走了？"他問。

這時莫雷爾太太站了起來，那個女侍應正從不遠的地方走過。

"給我們來一個提子餡餅，好嗎？"莫雷爾太太清楚地說道。

女侍應侮慢地回頭一顧。

"就來，"她說。

"我們已經等了好久，"莫雷爾太太說。

過了一會兒，那女孩端來了餡餅，莫雷爾太太冷冷地告訴她要結賬。保羅恨不得能鑽到地板底下。他對母親的強硬感到吃驚。他知道只有多年的磨練才使得她堅持自己的每一點權利。其實她也像他一樣感到心有餘悸。

從那家飯館出來，他們鬆了一口氣。"以後我再也不去那個鬼地方了！"她堅決地說。

（英）勞倫斯：《兒子與情人》

9 Lighting a Cigarette

Then he took out a tobacco pouch and a packet of papers and rolled himself a cigarette. He tried to make a lighter work and finally put it in his pocket and went over to the brazier, leaned over, reached inside, brought up a piece of charcoal, juggled it in one hand while he blew on it, then lit the cigarette and tossed the lump of charcoal back into the brazier.

Ernest Hemingway: <u>For Whom the Bell Tolls</u>

九　點煙

　　然後他掏出煙草袋和一包捲煙紙，捲了一支煙，用打火機打了幾下，沒打着，就乾脆把它放進口袋裏，走到火盆旁，彎下腰，將手伸入火盆，取出一塊炭，玩雜耍似地單手將它拋來拋去，又往上面吹氣，接着點燃捲煙後，又把那塊炭扔回了火盆。

　　　　　　　　　　　　（美）海明威《戰地鐘聲》

10 Playing the Fiddle

The old fiddle squeaks and shrieks in protest, but Tamoszius has no mercy. The sweat starts out on his forehead, and he bends over like a cyclist on the last lap of a race[1]. His body shakes and throbs like a runaway steam engine, and the ear cannot follow the flying showers of notes — there is a pale-blue mist[2] where you look to see his bowing arm. With a most wonderful rush he comes to the end of the tune, and flings up his hands and staggers back exhausted.

Upton Sinclair: The Jungle

---

1. last lap of a race：比賽的最後一段。

2. pale-blue mist：Tamoszius 穿着淺藍色的衣服，他拉弓的快速動作，使得手臂彷彿籠罩在淺藍色的霧中。

十　提琴演奏

　　那把舊小提琴吱吱尖叫着，好像在抗議，但塔莫修斯
毫不留情，汗珠從他的前額上滲出，他彎着身子，猶如在
最後衝刺的自行車運動員。他的身體像一台失控的蒸汽機
似的搖擺顫動，音符狂風暴雨般湧來，連耳朵都跟不上
了。朝着他那彎曲的，在拉弦的手臂望過去，只見一團淡
藍色的霧靄。他以極為奇妙的急速動作拉到曲終，雙手向
上一甩，精疲力盡地踉蹌幾步退了回去。

　　　　　　　　　　　（美）厄普頓·辛克萊：《屠場》

11 Playing the Piano

She kept her place at the piano, and I kept mine at the card-table. She played unintermittingly — played as if the music was her only refuge from herself. Sometimes her fingers touched the notes with a lingering fondness — a soft, plaintive, dying tenderness, unutterably beautiful and mournful to hear; sometimes they faltered and failed her, or hurried over the instrument mechanically, as if their task was a burden to them. But still, change and waver as they might in the expression they imparted to the music[1], their resolution to play never faltered[2].

Wilkie Collins: The Woman in White

---

1. the expression they imparted to the music：賦予音樂以感情。
   they：手指。
2. their resolution to play never faltered：their 指 "手指"；全句直譯為，手指彈奏下去的決心從未動搖過。

十一　彈鋼琴

　　她一直坐在鋼琴前，而我一直坐在牌桌邊。她不停地彈着琴 —— 彈琴的樣子彷彿只有音樂可以使她忘了自己。有時候，她的手指觸到琴鍵，流露出依依不捨的情調 —— 溫婉、哀怨、纏綿悱惻的柔情，聽起來無比優美而又傷感；有時候，手指頓了頓，沒有彈好，或者機械地在琴鍵上匆匆掠過，彷彿彈奏已經成為一種負擔。雖然十指在以音樂表達情感時偶爾會游移不定、躊躇不決，但絲毫沒有中止彈奏的意思。

　　　　　　　　　　（英）威爾基·柯林斯《白衣女人》

12   She Was Not Only Singing

The large room was full of people. One of the girls in yellow was playing the piano, and beside her stood a tall, red-haired young lady from a famous chorus, engaged in song. She had drunk a quantity of champagne, and during the course of her song she had decided, ineptly, that everything was very, very sad — she was not only singing, she was weeping too. Whenever there was a pause in the song she filled it with gasping, broken sobs, and then took up the lyric again in a quavering soprano. The tears coursed down her cheeks — not freely, however, for when they came into contact with her heavily beaded eyelashes they assumed an inky colour, and pursued the rest of their way in slow black rivulets. A humorous suggestion was made that she sing the notes on her face[1], whereupon she threw up her hands, sank into a chair, and went off into a deep vinous sleep[2].

F. Scott Fitzgerald: The Great Gatsby

---

1. the notes on her face：眼淚接觸到深色的眼影便染上了黑色，從臉上流過，很像樂譜上的音符。
2. a deep vinous sleep：酒後沉睡。

十二 哀歌

　　這個房間很大，裏面有很多人。一個身穿黃色衣服的女孩正在彈奏鋼琴，她身旁站着一位身材修長、紅頭髮的年輕女郎，正在引吭高歌，她是一個著名合唱團的團員。她喝了不少香檳，在演唱的過程中，刻意把每字每句都唱得十分悲切，讓人聽上去有些彆扭 —— 她不只是在唱歌，也是在哭泣。每到間歇處，她就上氣不接下氣地抽噎着，然後再用顫抖的高音繼續唱下去。她淚流滿面，但眼淚流得並不順暢 —— 她的睫毛沾滿了淚珠，所以眼淚碰到睫毛時，便染上了墨色，接着往下流的時候，就變成了一條條緩緩的、黑色的小溪。有人開玩笑說，希望她唱她臉上的譜子。聽到這話，她雙手向空中一甩，跌坐到一把椅子上，借着酒勁兒昏睡過去。

　　　　　　　　　　(美) 菲茨傑拉德：《燈綠夢緲》

13 Dancing As He Pleases

The company pairs off quickly, and the whole room is soon in motion. Apparently nobody knows how to waltz[1], but that is nothing of any consequence — there is music, and they dance, each as he pleases, just as before they sang. Most of them prefer the "two-step", especially the young people, with whom it is the fashion. The older people have dances from home, strange and complicated steps which they execute with grave solemnity[2]. Some do not dance anything at all, but simply hold each other's hands and allow the undisciplined joy of motion to express itself with their feet.

Upton Sinclair: The Jungle

---

1. to waltz：跳華爾茲舞。此時樂隊演奏的是 3/4 拍的華爾茲舞曲，應該跳三步舞。
2. execute with grave solemnity：十分嚴肅地跳着。execute：表演（動作等）。

十三　漫舞

　　大家很快找到了各自的舞伴，整個房間立刻充滿了漫舞的身影。顯然，大家都不會跳華爾茲，但這無關緊要，只要有音樂就可以了。大家隨心所欲地跳着，就像剛才隨心所欲地唱歌那樣。大多數人喜歡"二步舞"，特別是年輕人，他們時興跳這種舞。年長一些的人跳的是家鄉舞，他們一本正經地邁着古怪、複雜的步子。還有些人根本不是在跳舞，只不過是相互牽着手，毫無規則地移動着腳步，表現出無拘無束的喜悅心情。

　　　　　　　　　　　（美）厄普頓·辛克萊《屠場》

14   A Rolling Gait

He[1] walked at the other's heels with a swing to his shoulders, and his legs spread unwittingly, as if the level floors were tilting up and sinking down to the heave and lunge of the sea. The wide rooms seemed too narrow for his rolling gait, and to himself he was in terror lest his broad shoulders should collide with the doorways or sweep the bric-a-brac from the low mantel. He recoiled from side to side between the various objects and multiplied the hazards that in reality lodged only in his mind. Between a grand piano and a centre-table piled high with books was space for a half a dozen to walk abreast, yet he essayed[2] it with trepidation. His heavy arms hung loosely at his sides. He did not know what to do with those arms and hands, and when, to his excited vision, one arm seemed liable to brush against the books on the table, be lurched away like a frightened horse, barely missing the piano stool. He watched the easy walk of

---

1. He：文中主角馬丁・伊登是個二十歲的窮水手，這天來見朋友的家人。他生性敏感，又自慚形穢，因此感到局促不安行為舉止異常笨拙。

2. essayed：（文學用語）試圖，嘗試。

十四　搖搖擺擺

他跟在那人的後面走，雙肩一搖一擺的，兩條腿不知不覺地張開着，好像這平坦的地板正隨着海浪的起伏和湧動忽兒上升，忽兒下沉似的。他這種搖擺的步態使得這些寬敞的房間顯得十分狹窄。他還心懷恐懼，害怕自己寬寬的肩膀會撞到門框上，或者將低低的壁爐架上的小擺設給掃下來。他在各式各樣的物件中走着，左躲右閃，這一來平添了不少危險，其實這些危險只存在於他的想象之中。在一架大鋼琴和屋中央一張堆着高高一大疊書的桌子之間，有很大的空間，足夠五、六個人並肩走過，而他還是提心弔膽地走過去。他那兩條粗大的胳膊軟軟地垂在兩側。他不知道胳膊和手怎麼放才好。他心情興奮，一看到一隻胳膊似乎就要碰上桌子上的書本，就像一匹受驚的馬一樣往旁邊一閃，險些撞到那隻琴凳。他看見前面那人走

the other in front of him, and for the first time realized that his walk was different from that of other men. He experienced a momentary pang of shame that he should walk so uncouthly. The sweat burst through the skin of his forehead in tiny beads, and he paused and mopped his bronzed face with his handkerchief.

Jack London: Martin Eden

起路來從容不迫，才第一次意識到自己的步態與眾不同。
想想自己走路的樣子竟是那麼粗野，他不禁感到一陣慚
愧，前額上冒出一顆顆汗珠。於是他停下來，用手帕擦了
擦古銅色的臉。

　　　　　　　　　（美）傑克‧倫敦《馬丁‧伊登》

15 They Scuffled[1] Inch by Inch

They stepped uncomfortably from the safety of the plank platform and, balancing on their toes, taking cautious strides, ventured along the road. The sleety rain was turning to snow. The air was stealthily cold. Beneath an inch of water was a layer of ice, so that as they wavered with their suitcases they slid and almost fell. The wet snow drenched their gloves: the water underfoot splashed their itching ankles. They scuffled inch by inch for three blocks.

Sinclair Lewis: <u>Main Street</u>

---

1. scuffled ： ＝ shuffled，拖着腳步。

十五　步履艱難

　　站台的木地板走上去穩穩當當，出了站台就步履維艱
了。他們踮着腳尖，小心翼翼地邁着步子，冒着滑倒的危
險向前走着。剛才還下着冷雨，現在下起雪來。寒氣刺
骨。一英寸深的積水下面，結上一層冰，他們提着箱子，
走起來搖搖挽挽的，腳下一滑，險些跌倒。濕漉漉的雪弄濕
了他們的手套，腳下的水濺到發癢的腳踝上。他們一寸一
寸地挪動着腳步，好不容易走了三個街區。

　　　　　　　　　　　　　（美）辛克萊·路易斯：《大街》

16   Swinging through the Air

He set off with a spring, and in a moment was flying through the air, almost out of the door of the shed, ...

He was swinging through the air, every bit of him swinging, like a bird that swoops for joy of movement. And he looked down at her. Her crimson cap hung over her dark curls, her beautiful warm face, so still in a kind of brooding, was lifted towards him. It was dark and rather cold in the shed. Suddenly a swallow came down from the high roof and darted out of the door.

"I didn't know a bird was watching," he called.

He swung negligently. She could feel him falling and lifting through the air, as if he were lying on some force.

"Now I'll die," he said, in a detached, dreamy voice, as though he were the dying motion of the swing. She watched him, fascinated. Suddenly he put on the brake and jumped out.

D.H. Lawrence: <u>Sons and Lovers</u>

十六　蕩鞦韆

他一縱身蕩了起來，一下子蕩到了半空中，差一點飛出了牛棚……

他在空中蕩來蕩去，他身體的每個部分都在擺動，就像一隻小鳥在快樂地飛翔。他俯視着她，那頂深紅色的帽子罩在她黑黑的捲髮上，她抬着頭，那張臉美麗而熱情，在沉思中顯得十分安詳。牛棚裏暗暗的，而且很冷。忽然，一隻燕子從高高的屋頂上飛了下來，一下子飛出了門外。

"我不知道有一隻鳥在偷看。"

他隨意地蕩着。她感到他在空中飛上飛下，好像有甚麼力量在托着他。

"我要停下來了，"他用超然的、夢幻般的聲音說道，似乎他就是慢慢停下來的鞦韆。她出神地望着他。猛然間他停住了，跳了下來。

(英）勞倫斯：《兒子與情人》

17 Horse and Man

The industry[1] and movements of the rider were not less remarkable than those of the ridden. At each change in the evolutions[2] of the latter, the former raised his tall person in the stirrups; producing, in this manner, by the undue elongation[3] of his legs, such sudden growths and diminishings of the stature, as baffled every conjecture that might be made as to his dimensions. If to this be added the fact that, in consequence of the *ex parte*[4] application of the spur, one side of the mare appeared to journey faster than the other; and that the aggrieved flank[5] was resolutely indicated by unremitted flourishes[6] of a bushy tail, we finish the picture of both horse and man.[7]

James Fenimore Cooper: The Last of the Mohicans

---

1. industry：技能，機靈。此義現已不常用。
2. evolutions：動作，尤指特定的步法。
3. undue elongation：過度的伸展。
4. *ex parte*：（拉丁語）單方面的。
5. the aggrieved flank：被刺痛的一側。

十七　騎馬

　　騎師的技巧和姿勢和他的坐騎同樣出色。那匹馬每向前一躍，這個騎師便在馬鐙上挺直他高高的身軀，他長長的雙腿快速地一伸一縮，令他的身材忽高忽矮，使人猜想不到他到底有多高。而且，因為他只在一邊使用馬靴刺，那匹馬跑起來似乎一邊比另一邊快，毛茸茸的尾巴還不停地揮動着，可以明顯地看出馬的一側被刺痛了。關於這位騎師和他的坐騎，我們就描述到這裏。

　　(美) 詹姆斯·費尼莫·庫珀：《最後的莫希干人》

6.　unremitted flourishes: unremitted：不停地。flourish：揮舞；這裏指大力擺動。

7.　這個句子很長，它的基本結構是：If the fact that ... and that ... be added to this, we finish the picture ... 。"if"從句裏用的是倒裝句，因為主語 fact 後面有兩個很長的同位語從句。整句可分析為"如果加上〔關於馬因一邊被刺痛，跑得更快，等等的〕描述，騎師與馬的描述也就完結了。"

18   He Threw Off His Clothes and Entered the Water[1]

Reinhard continued along the shore. At a stone's throw from the land he perceived a white waterlily. All at once he was seized with the desire to see it quite close, so he threw off his clothes and entered the water. It was quite shallow; sharp stones and water plants cut his feet, and yet he could not reach water deep enough for him to swim in.

Then suddenly he stepped out of his depth: the water swirled above him, and it was some time before he rose to the surface again. He struck out with hands and feet and swam about in a circle until he had made quite sure from what point he had entered the water. And soon too he saw the lily again floating lonely among the large, gleaming leaves.

He swam slowly, lifting every now and then his arms out of the water so that the drops trickled down and sparkled in the moonlight. Yet the distance between him and the flower showed no signs of diminishing, while the shore, as he glanced back at it, showed behind him in a hazy mist that

---

1.   這裏敘述了一位年輕人頗具浪漫色彩的一次湖中探險，對他入水、湖中擊波、返回岸邊等一系列動作進行了生動的描寫。

十八　水中探險

　　萊因哈得繼續沿着湖邊走。在離岸一箭之遙的地方，他看到一朵白色的睡蓮。突然間他產生了一種慾望，想靠近看一看，他便脫了衣服，走到湖中。水淺淺的，尖尖的石頭和水草劃着他的雙腳，但他還沒有走到可以游泳的深水處。

　　忽然他進入了深水處，水在他頭頂上打轉，過了一會兒，他才又浮到水面上。他四肢一起划動，轉着圈游着，直到弄清楚他剛才的入水處。隨後，他很快又看到了那朵睡蓮在閃光的大葉子中間獨自漂浮着。

　　他慢慢游過去，不時地把雙臂伸出水面，水珠滴下來，在月光中閃爍着。然而他與那花的距離卻不見縮短，他回頭望去，在他身後，湖岸籠罩在朦朧的、愈來愈濃的

ever deepened. But he refused to give up the venture and vigorously continued swimming in the same direction.

At length he had come so near the flower that he was able clearly to distinguish the silvery leaves[2] in the moonlight; but at the same time he felt himself entangled in a net formed by the smooth stems of the water plants which swayed up from the bottom and wound themselves round his naked limbs.

The unfamiliar water was black all round about him, and behind him he heard the sound of a fish leaping. Suddenly such an uncanny feeling overpowered him in the midst of this strange element[3] that with might and main he tore asunder and swam back upon to land in breathless haste. And when from the shore he looked back upon the lake, there floated the lily on the bosom of the darkling water as far away and as lonely as before.

Theodor W. Storm: <u>Immensee</u>

---

2. leaves：花瓣。
3. this strange element：指這個湖。

夜霧之中。但他不願放棄這次探險，便繼續用力朝着同一方向游過去。

他終於游到了離花很近的地方，在月光下可以清楚地辨認出那些銀色的花瓣，就在這時候，他感到自己被一張網纏住了，那是湖底浮起的水草的滑莖纏繞住了他赤裸的肢體。

他周圍是一片陌生的湖水，黑蒙蒙的，在身後他聽到一條魚躍出水面的聲音。突然，一種可怕的感覺攫住了他，他感到周圍的湖水生疏而怪異，於是用盡全力掙脫開水草的纏繞，以最快的速度游回到岸邊。他從岸上再向湖面望去，那朵睡蓮還漂浮在黑蒙蒙的湖心上，仍然是那麼遙遠，那麼孤獨。

(德) 西奧多·施篤姆：《茵夢湖》

19   Drifting over the Sea[1]

We shared the hatch cover between us. We took turn
and turn about, one lying flat on the cover and resting, while
the other, submerged to the neck, merely held on with his
hands. For two days and nights, spell and spell[2], on the cover
and in the water, we drifted over the ocean. Toward the last
I was delirious most of the time; and there were times, too,
when I heard Otoo babbling and raving in his native tongue.
Our continuous immersion prevented us from dying of thirst,
though the sea water and the sunshine gave us the prettiest
imaginable combination of salt pickle and sunburn.

Jack London: "The Heathen"

---

1. 本選段描繪沉船後，"我"和另一位船客奧圖被迫在海上漂流的情景。
2. spell and spell：spell 原指一段連續的時間，也可解作輪班工作。這
   裏重複使用，是個反復修辭手法(reiteration)。試比較前面的 "took
   turn and turn about"，都解作輪流交替。

十九　海上漂流

　　我們分享着這塊艙板。兩個人輪着，一個人躺在上面休息，另一個浸在海水中，只把頭露出來，用手扶着木板。我們就這樣輪着，一個在板上，一個在水中，在海裏漂浮了兩天兩夜。到後來，我大部分時間都神智昏亂；有時候，我也會聽到奧圖用土話喃喃囈語。因為一直泡在海裏，我們不致於渴死，但是海水和陽光使我們得到可想象出的最漂亮的腌鹹菜乾模樣及曬斑。

（美）傑克‧倫敦：《異教徒》

20　I Decided Not to Struggle[1]

Scared and confounded as I was, I could not forbear going on with these Reflections[2]; when one of the Reapers approaching within ten Yards of the Ridge where I lay, made me apprehend that with the next Step I should be squashed to Death under his Foot, or cut in two with his Reaping Hook. And therefore when he was again about to move, I screamed as loud as Fear could make me. Whereupon the huge Creature trod short, and looking round about under him for some time, at last espied me as I lay on the Ground. He considered a while with the Caution of one who endeavours to lay hold on a small dangerous Animal in such a Manner that it shall not be able either to scratch or to bite him; as I my self have sometimes done with a Weasel in England. At length he ventured to take me up behind by the middle between his Fore-finger and Thumb, and brought me within three Yards of his Eyes, that he might behold my Shape more perfectly.

---

1. 這是格利佛初到大人國的一段冒險經歷。作者運用了幻想的手法，把虛構的情節描寫細緻逼真。
2. 這篇裏每個名詞的第一個字母都是大寫的。此外有些字的拼寫跟現代英語不同，如 my self、mean time、an humble... 等。

二十　化險為夷

　　我提心弔膽，不知所措，不禁這樣胡思亂想着，忽然一個割麥人走過來，離我躺着的田隴只有十碼遠，我擔心他再邁一步，就會把我踩死或者用鐮刀把我割成兩半。所以當他又要邁步的時候，我嚇得拼命大叫起來。那巨人聽到喊聲便猛地停下步子，在腳底下找來找去，最後終於發現了躺在地上的我。他遲疑了一會兒，那小心翼翼的樣子，就像一個想拿起一隻危險的小動物，又要防止被牠抓傷或咬傷的人，我在英國捉黃鼠狼的時候，也是這個樣子。最後，他從我的身後用食指和大拇指捏住我的腰部，把我提了起來，拿到離他的眼睛三碼遠的地方，以便更仔

I guessed his Meaning; and my good Fortune gave me so much Presence of Mind, that I resolved not to struggle in the least as he held me in the Air above sixty Foot from the Ground; although he grievously pinched my Sides, for fear I should slip through his Fingers. All I ventured was to raise mine Eyes towards the Sun, and place my Hands together in a supplicating Posture, and to speak some Words in an humble melancholy Tone, suitable to the Condition I then was in. For, I apprehended every Moment that he would dash me against the Ground, as we usually do any little hateful Animal which we have a Mind to destroy. But my good Star would have it, that he appeared pleased with my Voice and Gestures, and began to look upon me as a Curiosity; much wondering to hear me pronounce articulate Words, although he could not understand them. In the mean time I was not able to forbear Groaning and shedding Tears, and turning my Head towards my Sides; letting him know, as well as I could, how cruelly I was hurt by the Pressure of his Thumb and Finger. He seemed to apprehend my Meaning; for, lifting up the Lappet of his Coat, he put me gently into it, and immediately ran along with me to his Master, who was a substantial Farmer, and the same Person I had first seen in the Field.

Jonathan Swift: Gulliver's Travels

細地觀察我的模樣。我猜到了他的用意。他把我提到離地六十尺高的半空中，幸虧我能夠保持冷靜，我決定一點也不掙扎，他用力地捏着我的腰，怕我從指縫間溜掉。我只好仰面朝天，雙手合十，做出哀求的樣子，用適合我當時處境的、謙卑而悽慘的語調說了幾句話。因為我擔心他隨時會把我扔到地上，就像我們常常想弄死那些可惡的小動物那樣。但是我福星高照，他似乎喜歡我的聲音和手勢，開始把我當成一件奇物；他好奇地聽到我說出清晰的字語，雖然他並不懂。同時，我忍不住地呻吟流淚，用頭示意指向我的腰部，盡力讓他明白，他的兩個指頭把我捏得很痛。他好像明白了我的意思，提起上衣的下擺，輕輕地把我放進去，然後馬上帶着我跑去找他的主人，這位主人是個富裕的農夫，就是我當初在地裏看到的那位。

(英) 斯威夫特：《格列佛遊記》

21　He Ran Headlong at Me[1]

He ran headlong at me: I felt him grasp my hair and my shoulder: he had closed with[2] a desperate thing. I really saw in him a tyrant: a murderer. I felt a drop or two of blood from my head trickle down my neck, and was sensible of somewhat pungent suffering: these sensations for the time predominated over fear, and I received him in frantic sort. I don't very well know what I did with my hands, but he called me "Rat! rat[3]!"and bellowed out aloud. Aid was near him: Eliza and Georgiana had run for Mrs Reed, who was gone upstairs; she now came upon the scene, followed by Bessie and her maid Abbot. We were parted.

Charlotte Brontë: Jane Eyre

---

1. 簡·愛是父母雙亡的孤兒，生活在舅母里德太太家裏，表哥約翰常常虐待她。這一次她忍無可忍，便拼命地與他撕打起來。
2. closed with：與……搏鬥。close 的此種意義現已不常用。
3. rat：字面意義為"耗子"，英語中常用來罵人，但漢語中沒有此種用法，為了便於理解，漢譯中變換形象，採用形式有悖而功能對等的表達法，如"兔崽子"之類。

二十一　打架

　　他猛地向我衝過來。我感覺到他抓住了我的頭髮和肩膀。他是在跟一個亡命之徒決一死戰。我看他真像是一個暴君，一個殺人犯。我覺得有一、兩滴血從我的頭上順着脖子往下流，並且感到了幾分劇烈的痛楚。這些感覺一時壓倒了恐懼，我便拼命地跟他對打起來。我不太清楚自己的雙手幹了些甚麼，只聽到他在罵我："兔崽子！兔崽子！"同時大聲喊叫。援兵就在他身邊。伊麗莎和喬治娜跑去找了里德太太，她剛才去了樓上，現在來到了現場，後面還跟着蓓茜和她的使女阿博特。我們被拉開了……

　　　　　　　　　　(英) 夏洛蒂·勃朗特：《簡·愛》

22　Killing a Rat

A huge black rat squealed and leaped at Bigger's trouser-leg and snagged it in his teeth, hanging on.

"Goddamn!" Bigger whispered fiercely, whirling and kicking out his leg with all the strength of his body. The force of his movement shook the rat loose and it sailed through the air and struck a wall. Instantly, it rolled over and leaped again. Bigger dodged and the rat landed against a table leg. With clenched teeth, Bigger held the skillet; he was afraid to hurl it, fearing that he might miss. The rat squeaked and turned and ran in a narrow circle, looking for a place to hide; it leaped again past Bigger and scurried on dry rasping feet[1] to one side of the box and then to the other, searching for the hole. Then it turned and reared upon its hind legs.

"Hit 'im, Bigger!" Buddy shouted.

"Kill 'im!" the woman screamed.

The rat's belly pulsed with fear. Bigger advanced a step and the rat emitted a long thin song of defiance, its black beady eyes glittering, its tiny forefeet pawing the air

---

1.　dry rasping feet：指老鼠跑動時，乾乾的爪子刮擦地面而發出的聲音。

二十二 打老鼠

　　一隻碩大的黑色老鼠尖叫着，跳到比格的褲腿上，用牙齒牢牢地叼住不放。

　　"媽的！"比格狠狠地小聲罵道，他猛地一轉身，使盡全身力氣把那條腿踢出去。他這麼一用力，那隻老鼠被甩了出去，撞到牆上。可牠就地一滾，又竄了過來。比格一閃身，老鼠落到一隻桌腿旁。比格咬緊牙，手裏握着鐵鍋，不敢扔出去，怕打不着。老鼠吱吱叫着，轉過身來，兜着小圈跑，想找個地方藏身；牠又從比格身邊竄過去，撒開乾乾的爪子撲哧撲哧地衝到箱子一邊，又衝到另一邊，尋找洞口。接着牠轉過身，翹起兩隻前腿。

　　"打呀，比格！"布迪喊道。

　　"打死牠！"媽媽尖聲叫道。

　　老鼠的腹部因恐懼而不住地顫抖。比格向前邁了一步，老鼠發出一聲長長的尖叫，好像在唱一首挑戰之歌。牠那小黑珠似的眼睛閃動着，兩隻細細的前爪在空中亂抓

restlessly. Bigger swung the skillet; it skidded over the floor, missing the rat, and clattered to a stop against a wall.

"Goddamn!"

The rat leaped. Bigger sprang to one side. The rat stopped under a chair and let out a furious screak. Bigger moved slowly backward toward the door.

"Gimmie that skillet, Buddy," he asked quietly, not taking his eyes from the rat.

Buddy extended his hand. Bigger caught the skillet and lifted it high in the air. The rat scuttled across the floor and stopped again at the box and searched quickly for the hole; then it reared once more and bared long yellow fangs, piping[2] shrilly, belly quivering.

Bigger aimed and let the skillet fly with a heavy grunt. There was a shattering of wood as the box caved in[3]. The woman screamed and hid her face in her hands. Bigger tiptoed forward and peered.

"I got 'im," he muttered, his clenched teeth bared in a smile. "By God, I got 'im."

Richard Wright: <u>Native Son</u>

---

2. piping：似笛子的尖聲。

3. caved in：塌落，倒坍。

亂撬。比格把鐵鍋拋了出去，鐵鍋從地板上滑過，沒有擊
中老鼠，咣啷一聲撞在牆上。

"媽的！"

老鼠跳起來，比格一躍身閃到一邊。老鼠停在一把椅
子底下，發出一聲狂叫。比格慢慢地退到門口。

"給我鐵鍋，布迪。"他輕聲說，同時目不轉睛地盯
着老鼠。

布迪將鐵鍋遞給他，比格把鍋高高舉到空中。老鼠飛
快地從地板上跑過去，又停在箱子旁邊，迅速地尋找着洞
口。然後牠又翹起前爪，露出長長的、黃色的尖牙，尖聲
叫着，肚皮不停地顫抖。

比格瞄準了，重重地哼了一聲，把鐵鍋拋了出去。箱
子被砸爛了，木片散落開。媽媽尖叫一聲，用手摀住了
臉。比格躡手躡腳地走上前，悄悄地看了看。

"我打中了，"他咕噥道，咧嘴一笑，咬緊的牙齒露
了出來。"老天爺，我打中了。"

(美) 理查·賴特《土生子》

23　The Line Was Growing Rapidly[1]

The line was growing rapidly. Already there were fifty or more, and those at the head, by their demeanour, evidently congratulated themselves upon not having so long to wait as those at the foot. There was much jerking of heads, and looking down the line.

...

For the most part there was silence; gaunt men shuffling, glancing and beating their arms[2].

At last the door opened and the motherly-looking sister appeared. She only looked an order. Slowly the line moved up and, one by one, passed in, until twenty-five were counted. Then she interposed a stout arm, and the line halted, with six men on the steps. Of these the ex-manager[3] was one. Waiting thus, some talked, some ejaculated concerning the misery of

---

1. 本篇的背景是十九世紀末的紐約城，一羣窮困潦倒的人正在一個救濟機構(天主教的傳道所)前排隊，等着吃免費的午餐。
2. beating their arms：此時正值寒冬，這些動作是人體在寒冷時的條件反射。
3. ex-manager：前經理，這裏指隨後説到的赫斯伍得。

二十三　排隊

　　排隊的人數在迅速地增加，已經有五十多個人了。排在隊首的人想到後邊的人要等那麼久，便明顯地流露出慶幸的樣子。他們不停地回頭向後面張望。

　　……

　　排隊的人大多一言不發。他們面容憔悴，不停地跺着腳，甩動着胳膊，前後掃視着。

　　門終於打開了，出來一個慈眉善目的修女。她只用眼神示意了一下，隊伍開始慢慢地向前移動，一個一個地走進去。她數到二十五個，就伸出粗壯的胳膊一擋，隊伍停了下來，有六個人站在台階上，曾經做過經理的赫斯伍得也在其中。大家就這樣等待着，有人在交談，有人在唉聲

it; some brooded, as did Hurstwood. At last he was admitted, and, having eaten, came away, almost angered because of his pains in getting it.

Theodore Dreiser: Sister Carrie

嘆氣，也有人像赫斯伍得那樣在沉思。最後他終於被放了
進去，吃了飯便離開了。為吃一餐飯等得如此辛苦，他真
有些惱火。

　　　　　　　　(美) 德萊塞；《嘉利妹妹》

24　The Pandybat Came Down[1]

He banged his pandybat down on the desk and cried:
— Up, Fleming! Up, my boy!
Fleming stood up slowly.
— Hold out! cried the prefect of studies.
Fleming held out his hand. The pandybat came down on it with a loud smacking sound: one, two, three, four, five, six.
— Other hand!
The pandybat came down again in six loud quick smacks.
— Kneel down! cried the prefect of studies.
Fleming knelt down squeezing his hands under his armpits, his face contorted with pain ...

James Joyce: *A Portrait of the Artist as a Young Man*

---

1. 這是在天主教耶穌會辦的寄宿學校裏，學生受體罰的一個場面。在作文課上，學生弗萊明被老師罰跪，這時學監進來了，他又用打手棒處罰了弗萊明。本篇是作者喬伊斯時代英國社會流行的對犯規學生實施體罰的一個生動寫照。

二十四　體罰

他（學監）用打手棒在桌子上猛地一敲，喊道：

"站起來，弗萊明！站起來，孩子！"

弗萊明慢慢地站了起來。

"伸出手來！"學監喊道。

弗萊明伸出手，打手棒打在上面，發出很響的啪啪聲：一、二、三、四、五、六。

"另一隻手。"

打手棒又飛快地打了下來，連續六下，發出很響的聲音。

"跪下！"學監喊道。

弗萊明跪了下來，把兩手緊緊地夾在腋下，他的臉因痛苦而扭曲了……

(英) 喬伊斯：《藝術家年青時期的畫像》

25 The Purchase[1]

...In the store, they found that shine and rustle[2] of new things which immediately laid hold of Carrie's heart. Under the influence of a good dinner and Drouet's radiating presence, the scheme proposed[3] seemed feasible. She looked about and picked a jacket like the one which she had admired at The Fair. When she got it in her hand it seemed so much nicer. The saleswoman helped her on with it, and, by accident, it fitted perfectly. Drouet's face lightened as he saw the improvement. She looked quite smart.

"That's the thing," he said.

Carrie turned before the glass. She could not help feeling pleased as she looked at herself. A warm glow crept into her cheeks.

"That's the thing," said Drouet. "Now pay for it."

"It's nine dollars," said Carrie.

"That's all right — take it," said Drouet.

---

1. 本篇描寫嘉莉在男友的陪伴下，在商店裏挑選衣服。文字雖然不多，但從選衣、試穿到決定買衣、付款，描寫得十分完整，語言簡潔活潑。

2. shine and rustle：shine 這裏指耀眼生輝的貨品；rustle 這裏有新產品貨如輪轉的意味。

二十五　購衣

……在商店裏，琳琅滿目的時新商品把嘉莉深深地吸引住了。剛剛享用了一頓美餐，又加上德勞埃的熱心陪伴，嘉莉覺得他所提的購物計劃是可行的。她左看看，右看看，挑了一件外套，樣式很像她在展銷會上看中的那一件。一拿到手裏，她又感到這一件要漂亮得多。女店員幫她穿上，剛巧非常合身。德勞埃看到她整個人煥然一新；臉上便掛滿了笑容。她樣子很漂亮。

"這件正好，"他説。

嘉莉在鏡前轉來轉去，端詳着自己，禁不住滿心歡喜，雙頰緋紅。

"就買這件，"德勞埃説，"去付錢吧。"

"要九塊錢呢，"嘉莉説。

"沒關係 —— 買吧，"德勞埃説。

---

3. the scheme proposed：這裏指德勞埃提出的購物計劃。嘉莉剛剛從農村來到芝加哥，十分貧窮，德勞埃給了她二十塊錢，讓她添置一些衣物。嘉莉後來做了德勞埃的情人。

She reached in her purse and took out one of the bills.
The woman asked if she would wear the coat and went off.
In a few minutes she was back and the purchase was closed.

Theodore Dreiser: <u>Sister Carrie</u>

她把手伸進錢包，拿出一張鈔票。女店員問她是否要穿着走，然後就拿着錢走開了。不一會兒，她回來了，錢款已結清了。

　　　　　　　　　(美) 德萊塞：《嘉莉妹妹》

26   Nursing an Old Man[1]

Then she hoisted her tired body up and drew the comforter about her. She moved slowly to the corner and stood looking down at the wasted face, into the wide, frightened eyes. Then slowly she lay down beside him. He shook his head slowly from side to side. Rose of Sharon loosened one side of the blanket and bared her breast. "You got to," she said. She squirmed[2] closer and pulled his head close. "There!" she said. "There." Her hand moved behind his head and supported it. Her fingers moved gently in his hair. She looked up and across the barn, and her lips came together and smiled mysteriously.

John Steinbeck: The Grapes of Wrath

1. 產後不久的露斯莎倫遇到一個餓得奄奄一息的老人，他只有力氣吃流質食物了。露斯莎倫雖一貧如洗，但富有同情心。她決定用自己的乳汁來救活這位素不相識的老人。這一情節是美國經濟危機時期破產農民之間互助友愛精神的典型體現。

二十六　施捨乳汁

　　然後她拖着疲累的身子，站了起來。裹上那條蓋被，慢慢地走到角落裏，俯視着那張消瘦的臉，凝視着那雙睜得大大的、吃驚的眼睛。接着她慢慢地躺到他身邊。老人緩緩地搖着頭。露斯莎倫鬆開蓋被的一邊，露出乳房。"你得吃一點，"她說。她扭動身子靠近老人，把他的頭挪到身邊。"來，吃吧！"她說。她把手伸到他頭下面，托起來，又用手指輕輕地理着老人的頭髮。她看看倉棚的上面，又看看對面，抿起嘴唇，神秘地笑了。

　　　　　　　　　（美）斯坦貝克《憤怒的葡萄》

27　My Mouth Watered for It

About ten o'clock on the following morning, seedy and hungry, I was dragging myself along Portland Place, when a child that was passing, towed by a nursemaid, tossed a luscious big pear — minus one bite — into the gutter. I stopped, of course, and fastened my desiring eye on that muddy treasure. My mouth watered for it, my stomach craved it, my whole being begged for it[1]. But every time I made a move to get it some passing eye detected my purpose, and of course I straightened up, then, and looked indifferent, and pretended that I hadn't been thinking about the pear at all. This same thing kept happening and happening, and I couldn't get the pear. I was just getting desperate enough to brave all the shame, and to seize it, when a window behind me was raised, and a gentleman spoke out of it, saying:

"Step in here, please."

Mark Twain: The £ 1,000,000 Banknote

---

1. My mouth... begged for it：此處用了排比（parallelism）及層遞（gradation）手法，以加強效果。

二十七　垂涎欲滴

　　第二天上午十點左右，我衣衫襤褸、飢腸轆轆、步履艱難地走在波特蘭路的時候，剛好有一個小孩子由嫫姆牽着走過，他把一個大梨——只咬過一口的大梨——扔到了陰溝裏。不用說，我停下腳步，用貪婪的眼睛盯住那隻沾滿污泥的寶物。我嘴裏垂涎欲滴，肚子裏充滿了渴望，整個生命都在乞求它。但是我每次剛想動手去撿它，就有過路人的眼睛察覺到我的意圖，當然我就只好站直身子，擺出不屑一顧的樣子，假裝根本就不曾覬覦過那隻梨。這種情形反復出現，我始終無法得手。後來我簡直無可奈何，正想不顧一切體面去撿的時候，我身後的一扇窗戶忽然打開了，一位先生從那裏面喊道：

　　"請進來吧。"

（美）馬克·吐溫：《百萬英鎊》

28　I'm Hungry

Hunger came to his stomach; an icy hand reached down his throat and clutched his intestines and tied them into a cold, tight knot that ached. The memory of the bottle of milk Bessie had heated for him last night came back so strongly that he could almost taste it. If he had that bottle of milk now he would make a fire out of a newspaper and hold the bottle over the flame until it was warm. He saw himself take the top off the white bottle, with some of the warm milk spilling over his black fingers[1], and then lift the bottle to his mouth and tilt his head and drink. His stomach did a slow flip-flop[2] and he heard it growl. He felt in his hunger a deep sense of duty, as powerful as the urge to breathe, as intimate as the beat of his heart. He felt like dropping to his knees and lifting his face to the sky and saying: "I'm hungry!" He wanted to pull off his clothes and roll in the snow until something nourishing seeped into his body through the pores of his skin. He wanted to grip something in his hands so hard that it would turn to food. But soon his hunger left; soon he was taking it a little easier.

Richard Wright: Native Son

1.　black fingers：黑色的手指。這段描寫的是一個黑人男孩。

二十八 飢腸轆轆

　　他的胃部產生了飢餓感。一隻冰冷的手從他的喉嚨伸下去，抓住了腸子，將它們攥成了一個冰冷的死結，隱隱作痛。他想起了蓓西昨晚給他熱的那瓶奶，這一回憶十分鮮明、強烈，他幾乎嚐到了牛奶的味道。如果他現在有那麼一瓶奶，他就會用報紙生個火，把瓶子放在火燄上溫熱。他彷彿看到自己打開白瓶的蓋子，一些熱奶濺到了他黑色的手指上，接着他把瓶子舉到嘴邊，仰着頭喝下去。他的胃慢慢向後翻轉了一下，他聽到裏面咕嚕作響。從自己的飢餓中，他感到了一種深深的責任感，就像呼吸的慾望那樣強烈，像心跳那樣熟悉。他恨不得雙膝跪下，仰天大喊：“我餓啦！”他想把衣服脫掉，在雪地裏打滾，直到富有營養的東西通過毛孔滲入他的體內。他想把甚麼東西緊緊攥在手裏，把它變成食物。但飢餓感很快消失了；他馬上感到舒服了一些。

（美）理查‧賴特：《土生子》

---

2. flip-flop：美式英語用法，後手翻。

29 A Long Uninterrupted Soporific Drone

Next, the secretary rose and started to read the indictment. He read distinctly (though he mispronounced his *l*'s and *r*'s) in a loud voice, but so rapidly that the words ran into one another and formed a long uninterrupted soporific drone. The judges leaned now on one, now on the other arm of their chairs, now on the table or back in their seats; they closed their eyes and opened them again, and whispered among themselves. Several times one of the gendarmes repressed a yawn.

Lev Tolstoy: <u>Resurrection</u>

二十九　昏昏欲睡

接着，書記官站起來，開始宣讀起訴書。他的聲音洪亮清晰（雖然有時將 l 和 r 讀錯），但是唸的速度太快，所有的詞都連在一起，形成了一長串連綿不斷的、令人昏昏欲睡的嗡嗡聲。法官們一會兒倚在椅子這邊的扶手上，一會兒又倚在那邊的扶手上；一會兒趴在桌子上，一會兒又靠在椅背上；他們一會兒閉上眼睛，一會兒又睜開，還彼此交頭接耳。一個憲兵好幾次要張開嘴打哈欠，都強壓了下去。

（俄）托爾斯泰：《復活》

30   He Was Tired

At five o'clock the following day old Jolyon sat alone, a cigar between his lips, and on a table by his side a cup of tea. He was tired, and before he had finished his cigar he fell asleep. A fly settled on his hair, his breathing sounded heavy in the drowsy silence, his upper lip under the white moustache puffed in and out. From between the fingers of his veined and wrinkled hand the cigar, dropping on the empty hearth, burned itself out.

John Galsworthy: The Man of Property

三十　睏倦

　　第二天五點鐘左右，老喬里恩獨自坐着，嘴裏夾着雪茄，身旁的桌子上放着一杯茶。他累了，雪茄還沒抽完就睡着了。一隻蒼蠅飛落在他的頭髮上。在一片沉寂中，他的呼吸顯得很粗重，長滿白鬍子的上唇隨着他的呼吸一起一落。他的手青筋暴露，佈滿皺紋，雪茄從他的指縫中掉到空空的壁爐上，已經燃盡了。

（英）高爾斯華綏：《有產者》

31   The Pilgrims Slept[1]

Below the roof of awnings, ... the pilgrims of an exacting faith[2] slept on mats, on blankets, on bare planks, on every deck, in all the dark corners, wrapped in dyed cloths, muffled in soiled rags, with their heads resting on small bundles, with their faces pressed to bent forearms: the men, the women, the children; the old with the young, the decrepit with the lusty — all equal before sleep, death's brother.

... The well-to-do had made for their families shelters with heavy boxes and dusty mats; the poor reposed side by side with all they had on earth tied up in a rag under their heads; the lone old men slept, with drawn-up legs upon their prayer-carpets, with their hands over their ears and one elbow on each side of the face; a father, his shoulders up and his knees under his forehead, dozed dejectedly by a boy who slept on his back with tousled hair and one arm commandingly extended; a woman covered from head to foot, like a corpse, with a piece of white sheeting, had a naked child in the hollow of each arm;...

Joseph Conrad: <u>Lord Jim</u>

1.　八百名旅客乘船前往麥加朝聖，這裏描述了他們在船上沉睡時各種各樣的姿態。

三十一　睡態

　　在船蓬下面，那些信仰嚴刻的宗教的朝聖者們睡着
了，睡在席子上、毯子上和光板上，睡在每一層甲板和每
一個陰暗角落裏，他們用染色布包着，用破舊骯髒的衣服
裏着，頭枕在小包裏上，臉靠在彎曲的前臂上：男人、女
人、孩子、老的、少的、衰弱的、強壯的——在死神的兄
弟睡神面前，人人平等。

　　……有錢人家用重重的箱子和滿是灰塵的席子做成個
臨時棲身處，窮人則一個挨一個地躺着，把所有家當綑在
破布裏當枕頭；孤獨的老人們縮起雙腿，睡在祈禱用的地
毯上，他們兩手抱着耳朵，兩臂夾着臉；一個做父親的縮
着脖子，頭枕膝蓋，一副有氣無力的樣子，在打瞌睡；他
的兒子靠在他的背上，頭髮蓬亂，伸着一隻胳膊，像在發
號施令。一個女人從頭到腳蓋着白被單，像具屍體，她兩
邊的胳肢窩裏，各睡着一個赤着身子的小孩；……

（英）康拉德：《吉姆爺》

2.　an exacting faith：嚴刻的信仰，此處指伊斯蘭教。

32   Open Your Eyes[1]

"It's always more like a fit than a nap," says Mr. Guppy, shaking him again, "Halloa, your lordship! Why, he might be robbed, fifty times over! Open your eyes!"

After much ado, he opens them, but without appearing to see his visitors, or any other objects. Though he crosses one leg on another, and folds his hands, and several times closes and opens his parched lips, he seems to all intents and purposes as insensible as before.

"He is alive, at any rate," says Mr. Guppy. "How are you, my Lord Chancellor. I have brought a friend of mine, sir, on a little matter of business."

The old man still sits, often smacking his dry lips without the least consciousness. After some minutes, he makes an attempt to rise. They help him up, and he staggers against the wall, and stares at them.

"How do you do, Mr. Krook?" says Mr. Guppy, in some discomfiture. "How do you do, sir? You are looking charming, Mr. Krook. I hope you are pretty well?"

---

1. 本篇描述一位老人從沉睡中清醒過來的緩慢過程，語言生動詼諧。

三十二　醒來

　　"他不是在睡覺，很可能是昏過去了，"格皮先生説着，又搖了搖他，"喂，大法官閣下！老天爺，即使有人來這裏偷上五十幾次東西，他都不會知道！睜開眼睛啊！"

　　克魯克先生好不容易才睜開了眼睛，但似乎看不見來訪者或其它的甚麼東西。雖然他蹺起了二郎腿，又把兩手握在一起，兩片乾裂的嘴唇張開合上了好幾次，他實際上仍然像剛才一樣不省人事。

　　"不管怎麼樣，他還活着，"格皮先生説，"你好嗎，大法官閣下？我帶來了一個朋友，先生，想跟您談點兒事兒。"

　　老頭還是坐在那裏，不時地咂着乾乾的嘴唇，毫無知覺。過了幾分鐘，他試着站起來。他們扶他起身，他蹣跚地靠着牆，瞪着他們。

　　"您好嗎，克魯克先生？"格皮略帶尷尬地説，"您好，先生！您氣色好極了，克魯克先生。您身體還不錯吧？"

The old man, in aiming a purposeless blow at Mr. Guppy, or at nothing, feebly swings himself round, and comes with his face against the wall. So he remains for a minute or two, heaped up against it; and then staggers down the shop to the front door. The air, the movement in the court, the lapse of time, or the combination of these things, recovers him. He comes back pretty steadily, adjusting his fur cap on his head, and looking keenly at them.

Charles Dickens: <u>Bleak House</u>

老頭不知是朝着格皮先生，還是朝着其它甚麼地方，毫無目的地揮了揮拳頭，有氣無力、搖搖挸挸地轉過身來，把臉貼在牆上；這樣呆了一、兩分鐘，他又頂着牆直起身來，踉踉蹌蹌地向店的前門走去。過了一陣子，新鮮空氣和院子裏的動靜使他漸漸清醒過來。他走回來的時候步履穩健，他正了正頭上的皮帽，目光銳利地看着他們。

（英）狄更斯：《荒涼山莊》

33 Cough[1]

From Lennie's little box of a chest there came a sound as though something was boiling. There was a great lump of something bubbling in his chest that he couldn't get rid of. When he coughed, the sweat sprang out on his head; his eyes bulged, his hands waved, and the great lump bubbled as a potato knocks in a saucepan. But what was more awful than all was when he didn't cough he sat against the pillow and never spoke or answered, or even made as if he heard. Only he looked offended.

Katherine Mansfield: "Life of Ma Parker"

---

1. 本篇描寫病人的 "咳嗽"。文中使用 "boiling"、"bubbling"
    "lump"、"bulged"、"as a potato knocks in a saucepan" 等詞語，
    比喻形象生動，把 "咳嗽" 的動作與感受描繪得淋漓盡致。

三十三　咳嗽

倫尼小小的胸腔裏發出一種聲音，好像有甚麼東西煮沸了。有個大硬塊在他的胸部咕嚕作響，他又吐不出來。他咳嗽的時候，頭上冒汗，眼睛圓睜，雙手也隨着抖動，那一大塊東西咕嚕咕嚕的，就像一個馬鈴薯在鍋裏蹦來蹦去。但最可怕的是他不咳嗽的時候，他靠着枕頭坐着，一聲不吭，誰叫他也不應聲，甚至作出聽不見的樣子。好像有人欺負了他。

　　(英) 凱瑟琳·曼斯菲爾德：《帕克大娘的一生》

34 Managing to Get out of Bed

Martin was not used to sickness, and when Maria and her little girl left him, he essayed to get up and dress. By a supreme exertion of will, with reeling brain and eyes that ached so that he could not keep them open, he managed to get out of bed, only to be left stranded[1] by his senses upon the table. Half an hour later he managed to regain the bed[2] where he was content to lie with closed eyes and analyze his various pains and weaknesses.

Jack London: Martin Eden

---

1. be left stranded：陷入困境，難以行動。

三十四　病中起身

　　馬丁不習慣生病，等瑪麗亞和她的小女一離開，他就試圖起身，想穿上衣裳。但他頭發暈，眼睛疼得睜都睜不開，他竭盡全力，才從牀上爬起來，可是又因體力不支，癱倒在桌子上。半個小時之後，他才勉強返回牀上，安心地閉上眼睛躺着，思忖着自己的種種病痛和虛弱的症狀。

　　　　　　　　　（美）傑克·倫敦：《馬丁·伊登》

35　She Was Pregnant and Careful

Beside them, clinging lightly to the bars, stood Rose of Sharon, and she balanced, swaying on the balls of her feet[1], and took up the road shock in her knees and hams. For Rose of Sharon was pregnant and careful. Her hair, braided and wrapped around her head, made an ash-blond crown. Her round soft face, which had been voluptuous and inviting a few months ago, had already put on the barrier[2] of pregnancy, the self-sufficient smile, the knowing perfection-look; and her plump body — full soft breasts and stomach, hard hips and buttocks that had swung so freely and provocatively as to invite slapping and stroking — her whole body had become demure and serious. Her whole thought and action were directed inward on the baby. She balanced on her toes now, for the baby's sake. And the world was pregnant to her[3]; she thought only in terms of reproduction and of motherhood.

John Steinbeck: The Grapes of Wrath

1.　balls of her feet：腳掌近大拇趾根部分。
2.　barrier：屏障，防綫；這裏是相對於前句的 inviting（誘人）而言。

三十五　孕婦乘車

　　露斯莎倫輕輕抓着橫杆，站在他們身旁，盡力保持平衡，她踮着腳尖，身體搖擺着，以膝部、大腿和臀部承受着一路的顛簸。她懷孕了，所以變得小心翼翼。她的頭髮梳成辮子盤在頭上，好像一頂淺金色的皇冠。她那圓潤嬌嫩的臉龐，幾個月前還性感誘人，現在則顯出了孕期的儀容，自滿的微笑，自覺完美的神情。還有她胖胖的身子——那柔軟豐滿的乳房、腹部和結實的臀部，曾是那麼誘人地、自由自在地捉動着，讓人禁不住要去拍一拍，摸一摸——現在她的整個身體都變得端莊而穩重了。她的所思所想，一舉一動都以腹中的胎兒為中心。為了胎兒的安全，她踮起腳尖。對她來説，整個世界就是懷孕，她腦子裏只有生育和做母親的念頭。

　　　　　　　　(美) 斯坦貝克：《憤怒的葡萄》

3.　the world was pregnant to her：這裏運用了誇張的手法，有力地刻劃了這位未來母親的心態——她心裏想的只有腹中的小生命。

36　Fierce Pains

The walking women had stopped. Rose of Sharon had stiffened, and she whined with pain. They laid her down on the mattress and wiped her forehead while she grunted and clenched her fists. And Ma talked softly to her. "Easy," Ma said. "Gonna[1] be all right — all right. Jus' grip ya han's[2]. Now, then, take your lip inta[3] your teeth. Tha's[4] good — tha's good." The pain passed on. They let her rest awhile, and then helped her up again, and the three walked back and forth, back and forth between the pains.

...

The pains were coming close now, twenty minutes apart. And Rose of Sharon had lost her restraint. She screamed fiercely under the fierce pains.

John Steinbeck: <u>The Grapes of Wrath</u>

1.　Gonna（美式口語）＝ going to.

2.　Jus' grip ya han's ＝ Just grip your hands.

3.　inta ＝ into

4. Tha's ＝ That's

三十六　產痛

　　那幾個踱步的女人停下腳步。露斯莎倫四肢僵硬，痛苦地嗚咽着。她們讓她躺在牀墊上，給她擦擦前額，她呻吟着，握緊了拳頭。媽柔聲地跟她說着話。"不要緊，"媽說，"很快就會好的——就好了。握緊拳頭，用牙齒咬住嘴唇。這樣就好了——很好了。"疼痛過去了。她們讓她休息了一會兒，然後又扶她起身。三個人在產婦陣痛的間歇中走來走去，走來走去。
　　……
　　現在陣痛越來越緊了，間隔為二十分鐘，露斯莎倫再也控制不住自己了。她在劇痛中大聲尖叫着。

　　　　　　　　　　　　（美）斯坦貝克：《憤怒的葡萄》

37   It Had Made Him Drunk[1]

He began to get into bed.... A temporary inability to raise his second foot onto the bed let him know what had been the secondary effect of drinking all that water[2]: it had made him drunk. This became a primary effect[3] when he lay in bed.... He reached up and turned off the light by the hanging switch above his head. The room began to rise upwards from the right-hand bottom corner of the bed, and yet seemed to keep in the same position. He threw back the covers and sat on the edge of the bed, his legs hanging. The room composed itself to rest. After a few moments he swung his legs back and lay down. The room lifted. He put his feet to the floor. The room stayed still. He put his legs on the bed but didn't lie down. The room moved. He sat on the edge of the bed. Nothing. He put one leg up on the bed. Something. In fact a great deal. He was evidently in a highly critical condition.

Kingsley Amis: <u>Lucky Jim</u>

---

1. 這一段極為生動地描寫了狄克遜醉酒時的幻覺 —— 他一變換姿勢，房子的位置也隨之變動。

2. drinking all that water：狄克遜先喝了半瓶紅葡萄酒，然後又喝了很多水。

三十七　醉酒

　　他開始上牀。……他把一條腿伸到牀上，伸另一條腿卻一時感到很困難，這時，他才知道喝了那麼多水以後所產生的副作用：他給灌醉了。而當他躺倒在牀上時，副作用就已經明顯見效了。……他伸出手，拉住吊在頭上的開關，把燈熄了。頓時，牀鋪右下角的那一邊房子開始往上升，但又似乎是原地未動。他掀開被單，坐到牀邊，兩腳懸空。房子安定了，不動了，過了一刻，他收回腿，躺下去，房子又往上升。他把腳伸到地板上，房子穩住了。他把腿縮到牀上，但不躺下，房子便左右移動。他又坐到牀沿上，一切安然無恙。他把一條腿放在牀上，感到房子有點變化。說實在的，有很大變化。很明顯，他醉得很厲害。

　　　　　　　（英）金斯萊·艾米斯：《幸運的吉姆》

3.　primary effect：(主要作用)與 secondary effect (副作用)是個對比；
　　這裏的意思是，過量的水在狄克遜身上產生的副作用變成了明顯的，
　　強烈的主要作用 —— 他醉了。

38   An Appalling Spasmodic Whooping-cough Dance[1]

I couldn't keep my eyes off him[2]. Always holding tight by the leg of the table with my hands and feet, I saw the miserable creature finger his glass playfully, take it up, smile, throw his head back, and drink the brandy off. Instantly afterwards, the company were seized with unspeakable consternation, owing to his springing to his feet, turning round several times in an appalling spasmodic whooping-cough dance, and rushing out at the door; he then became visible through the window, violently plunging and expectorating, making the most hideous faces, and apparently out of his mind.

Charles Dickens: Great Expectations

---

1. 本篇描繪人在嗆酒時的情景，文學作品對此類行為描繪不多，因此本選段的描寫很是難得。

2. "我"在酒裏摻了柏油水，擔心被發現，因此十分緊張，目不轉睛地盯着"他"。

三十八　嗆酒

　　我目不轉睛地盯着他，手腳緊緊地鈎住桌腿，只見這個可憐的傢伙把酒杯摩挲把玩了一會兒，拿起杯子，微笑着，一仰頭，將白蘭地一飲而盡。酒一入口，他便一下子跳了起來，一陣陣猛烈地咳嗽着，手舞足蹈地轉了幾圈，像是百日咳發作，樣子很嚇人；他衝出門外，在座的人都驚恐萬分。接着他出現在窗口，咳得踉踉蹌蹌，口吐白沫，做出種種可怕的表情，活像是精神錯亂。

　　　　　　　　　　　　(英) 狄更斯：《遠大前程》

39 No Sensation Was Aroused in the Hands[1]

The man looked down at his hands in order to locate them, and found them hanging on the ends of his arms. It struck him as curious that one should have to use his eyes in order to find out where his hands were. He began threshing his arms back and forth, beating the mittened hands against his sides. He did this for five minutes, violently, and his heart pumped enough blood up to the surface to put a stop to his shivering. But no sensation was aroused in the hands. He had an impression that they hung like weights on the ends of his arms, but when he tried to run the impression down, he could not find it.

Jack London: "To Build a Fire"

---

1. 本段描繪了一個人在北極圈附近的冰天雪地中雙手凍僵時的感覺。語言新穎幽默。

三十九　酷寒

那人低下頭去找自己的手，看到那兩隻手掛在胳膊的末端。他感到很奇怪，一個人居然要用眼睛來確定自己的手在哪裏。他開始前後甩動胳膊，並用帶手套的手敲打着兩肋。就這樣，他做了五分鐘的劇烈活動，心臟終於把足夠的血液抽到了身體的外層，他不再顫抖了。然而，手上仍然沒有知覺。在他的印象中，手像秤砣似的垂在雙臂下面。他順着胳膊尋找這種感覺的時候，卻沒有找到。

（美）傑克・倫敦：《生火》

40   She Passed from Death unto Life[1]

The large blue eyes unclosed, — a smile passed over her face; — she tried to raise her head, and to speak.

"Do you know me, Eva?"

"Dear papa," said the child, with a last effort, throwing her arms about his neck. In a moment they dropped again; and, as St. Clare raised his head, he saw a spasm of mortal agony[2] pass over the face, — she struggled for breath, and threw up her little hands.

...

The child lay panting on her pillows, as one exhausted, — the large clear eyes rolled up and fixed. Ah, what said those eyes, that spoke so much of heaven? Earth was past, and earthly pain; but so solemn, so mysterious, was the triumphant brightness of that face, that it checked even the sobs of sorrow. They pressed around her, in breathless stillness.

...

---

1. passed from death unto life：指小姑娘雖然死去了，但卻獲得了新的生命。

2. mortal agony：亦可解作人類能感受的痛苦。

四十　死亡

　　那雙藍色的大眼睛睜開了，她的臉上閃現出一絲微笑，她想抬起頭，想説話。

　　"你認得我嗎，伊娃？"

　　"親愛的爸爸，"孩子用最後一絲氣力説道，她摟住爸爸的脖子。不一會兒，她的手臂鬆開了。聖·克萊亞抬起頭，看到伊娃的面孔因一陣致命的痛楚而抽搐着。她喘不過氣來，憋得將兩隻小手舉向空中。

　　……

　　小姑娘躺在枕頭上喘着氣，好像一個精疲力竭的人，清澈透明的大眼睛向上翻着，一動不動。那雙顯示天意的大眼睛在訴説甚麼呢？她已超脱了塵世，超脱了塵世的痛苦，她臉上那凱旋的光輝多麼莊嚴，多麼神秘，這光輝使人停住了悲痛的嗚咽。大家圍上前來屏住呼吸，鴉雀無聲。

　　……

A bright, a glorious smile passed over her face, and she said, brokenly, — "O! love, — joy, — peace!" gave one sigh, and passed from death unto life!

Harriet Beecher Stowe: <u>Uncle Tom's Cabin</u>

伊娃的臉上浮現出光輝燦爛的微笑，她斷斷續續的
說，“哦！愛 —— 快樂 —— 和平！”，然後嘆息了一
聲，就越過了死亡，進入了永生！

　　(美) 哈里葉特‧比徹‧斯托：《湯姆大伯的小屋》

41　Keep an Eye on the Gold

Finally, the last agony began, days during which the old man's powerful frame battled with the forces of destruction[1]. He insisted on remaining seated near his fireplace, facing the door to the study. He pulled all the covers that were put over him into his lap, rolling them up and telling Nanon,

"Here, lock this up, don't let anyone steal it."

When he was able to open his eyes, in which the last sparks of life had taken refuge, he would immediately turn toward the door to his study where his treasures lay hidden, and say to his daughter:

"Are they there? Are they there?" in a voice that betrayed[2] a kind of panic.

"Yes, father."

"Keep an eye on the gold! ... Put some gold in front of me!"

Eugénie would spread some *louis*[3] out on a table before him, and he would stare at them for hours on end, like a baby

---

1.　forces of destruction：指死亡。
2.　betrayed：流露，表現。

四十一　守財奴之死

臨終的痛苦終於降臨了，那幾天葛朗台老頭結實的身子同毀滅性的力量抗爭着。他堅持要坐在壁爐旁邊，面對着密室的門。他把身上所有的蓋毯都拉到膝上，捲起來，對拿儂說，

"來，把這些鎖起來，別讓人偷走了。"

彌留之際的生命火花都殘存在他的眼睛裏，他一旦能夠睜開眼睛，就馬上轉向藏着財寶的密室的門，對女兒說：

"在那裏嗎？在那裏嗎？"聲音中帶着幾分恐慌。

"在那裏呢，父親。"

"看住金子！……拿些金子來，放在我面前！"

歐也妮把一些金路易攤在他面前的桌子上，老頭就連續幾個鐘頭盯着那些金子，就像一個剛剛學會看東西的嬰

---

3. *louis*：= *louis d'or*，金路易，法國古幣名。

who is just learning to see and who stupidly fixes his eyes upon a single object, and, like the baby, he would give a wry smile.

"It warms my heart," he would say now and then, letting an expression of beatitude steal over his face.

When the parish priest came to administer the last rites[4], his eyes, which had appeared to be lifeless for the last few hours, became animated again at the sight of the cross, the candlesticks, the silver basin of holy water, each of which he stared at intently, as the wen on his nose twitched for the last time. When the priest brought the gilded crucifix close to his lips so that he could kiss the figure of Christ, he made a fearful effort to grab it, and this final gesture cost him his life. He called out to Eugénie, whom he could not see, even though she was kneeling before him, her tears bathing his already cold hand.

"Father, give me your blessing," she asked.

"Take good care of everything! You will render an account to me up there[5]," he said, demonstrating, by these last words, that Christianity is the proper religion for misers.

Honoré de Balzac: <u>Engénie Grandet</u>

---

4. last rites：（給臨死的人做的）臨終聖禮。

5. render an account... up there：up there 指天國。這裏影射基督教的教義指人死後要向上帝報賬。

兒，呆呆地看着某一件物品，然後又像個嬰兒似的，怪怪地一笑。

"這樣我心裏就暖暖的，"他不時地這樣嘀咕着，臉上浮現出一片幸福的表情。

當教區牧師來做臨終法事時，他那雙前幾個小時都已毫無生氣的眼睛，一看到十字架、燭台和鑲銀的聖水壺，馬上又變得靈活起來，目不轉睛地盯着每一件法器，鼻子上的粉瘤也最後抽搐了一下。牧師把鑲金的十字架放到他唇邊，想讓他吻一吻耶穌的聖像，他卻作了一個嚇人的動作，要伸手去抓那個十字架，這個最後的姿勢要了他的命。他把歐也妮叫過來，雖然她已跪在他身邊，眼淚浸濕了他已經冰冷的手，他卻看不見她。

"父親，祝福我吧！"她請求道。

"料理好所有的事情，到那上邊向我報賬，"他說，這最後一句話證明，基督教應該是守財奴的宗教。

(法) 巴爾扎克：《歐也妮·葛朗台》

42   A Ripple of Laughter[1]

At some opinion of dirty Knowles, delivered with an air of supernatural cunning, a ripple of laughter ran along, rose like a wave, burst with a starting roar. They stamped with both feet; they turned their shouting faces to the sky; many, spluttering, slapped their thighs; while one or two, bent double, gasped, hugging themselves with both arms like men in pain. The carpenters and boatswain, without changing their attitude[2], shook with laughter where they sat; ... the cook was wiping his eyes with a greasy rag; and lame Knowles, astonished at his own success, stood in their midst showing a slow smile.

Joseph Conrad: The Nigger of the "Narcissus"

---

1. 本選段描寫 "水仙號" 船上因一位船員的滑稽講話而引起的一場大笑。
   作者用輕快的筆調,把人們大笑時的種種姿勢和神態刻劃得淋漓盡
   致。
2. without changing their attitude : 沒有變換姿勢。

四十二　大笑

髒漢諾爾斯發表了一通議論，他那一副狡點神秘的樣子，逗得大家哄堂大笑，笑聲像一排波浪奔湧、咆哮而過。他們跺着腳，笑得前仰後合；很多人噴着唾沫星子，拍着大腿；還有一、兩位笑彎了腰，上氣不接下氣的，雙臂捂着肚子，好像疼痛難忍。木匠和水手長坐在原地沒動，也笑得渾身顫抖；……廚子在用一塊油乎乎的布擦着眼睛；瘸腿的諾爾斯站在當中，沒想到自己的一番話會帶來這麼好的效果，愣了片刻，隨後也露出了笑容。

(英) 康拉得：《“水仙號”上的黑人》

43   A Frantic Fit of Laughing[1]

Arthur looked up. All the life and expression had gone out of his face; it was like a waxen mask.

"D-don't you think," he said softly, with a curious stammering hesitation on the words "th-that — all this — is — v-very — funny?"

...

Arthur suddenly threw back his head, and burst into a frantic fit of laughing.

"Arthur!" exclaimed the shipowner[2], rising with dignity, "I am amazed at your levity."

There was no answer but peal after peal of laughter, so loud and boisterous that even James began to doubt whether there was not something more the matter here than levity.

"Just like a hysterical woman," he muttered, turning, with a contemptuous shrug of his shoulders, to tramp impatiently up and down the room. "Really, Arthur, you're worse than Julia[3]; there, stop laughing! I can't wait about here all night."

---

1. 牛虻出獄後，他的同母異父兄弟詹姆斯認為他給家庭帶來了恥辱，要求他離開這個家。詹姆斯還告訴牛虻，他是個私生子，他的生父是蒙塔里尼神父。牛虻大受刺激，狂笑不止。

四十三　狂笑

亞瑟抬起頭來。他的臉變得毫無生氣，毫無表情，就像一副蠟製的假面具。

"你……你不覺得……這……這些……都很滑稽嗎？"他喃喃的説，吞吞吐吐的，樣子怪怪的。

……

亞瑟突然仰起頭，爆發出一陣瘋狂的大笑。

"亞瑟！"詹姆斯生氣地站起來喊道，"看你滿不在乎的樣子，真讓我吃驚。"

亞瑟沒有回答，只是一陣接一陣地大笑着，笑得很響很狂，詹姆斯不由得心生疑慮，他也許並非滿不在乎，而是有甚麼不妥吧。

"活像個歇斯底里的女人，"詹姆斯嘟囔着，他輕蔑地聳聳肩，轉過身，不耐煩地在房間裏來回踱步。"真的，亞瑟，你比朱麗亞還糟糕。喂，別笑了！我不能在這兒等你一晚上。"

---

2. shipowner：輪船公司的老闆，這裏指詹姆斯。翻譯時根據漢語表達習慣，把"輪船公司老闆"替換成"詹姆斯"，可以避免誤解。

3. Julia：詹姆斯的妻子，脾氣暴躁。

He might as well have asked the crucifix to come down from its pedestal[4]. Arthur was past caring for remonstrances or exhortations; he only laughed, and laughed, and laughed without end.

E . L . Voynich: <u>The Gadfly</u>

---

4. He might... pedestal：本句的意思是亞瑟根本不可能停止大笑。亞瑟的房間裏有個耶穌十架受難像，他經常跪在前面禱告。

這個要求簡直等於讓耶穌十架像自己從底座上走下來。亞瑟毫不理會他的抗議或規勸；他只是在笑，笑，不停地笑。

(英) 伏尼契：《牛虻》

44　A Fit of Hysterics[1]

There was a pause; then she came waveringly forward, put her hands on his shoulders, and seemed to collapse, or be dragging him, on to the bed. Unregarded, her spectacles fell off. She was making a curious noise, a steady, repeated, low-pitched moan that sounded as if it came from the pit of her stomach, as if she'd been sick over and over again and still wanted to be sick. Dixon half-helped, half-lifted her on to the bed. Now and then she gave a quiet, almost skittish little scream. Her face was pushed hard against his chest. Dixon didn't know whether she was fainting, or having a fit of hysterics, or simply breaking down and crying. Whatever it was he didn't know how to deal with it. When she felt that she was sitting on the bed next to him she threw herself forward so that her face was on his thigh. In a moment he felt moisture creeping through to his skin. He tried to lift her, but she was immovably heavy; her shoulders were shaking more rapidly than seemed to him normal even in a

---

1. a fit of hysterics：attacks of hysteria 歇斯底里發作。狄克遜告訴瑪格麗特，他們之間的關係已經不復存在了，一時間瑪格麗特的感情失控了。

四十四　歇斯底里

　　兩人都停住沒說話；過了一會兒，她搖搖挻挻走上前來，把手搭在他的肩膀上，並且好像要往牀上倒了似的，或許是在拉他上牀吧。她的眼鏡從鼻子上掉下來，她連理也不理。她在發出一種奇怪的聲音，一種平穩不變、反復不斷、低沉的呻吟聲，聽上去彷彿來自她的心窩，彷彿她嘔吐了許多次以後還想吐似的。狄克遜連扶帶挾地把她送到牀上。她不時地發出一聲低微的、幾乎是羞怯的、短暫的尖叫，臉緊貼着他的胸部。狄克遜不知道她是頭發暈，是歇斯底里，還是情不自禁地痛哭。不管是怎麼回事，他都對付不了。當她感到她已挨着他坐在牀上的時候，她便一下往前撲去，臉趴在他的大腿上。不一會兒，他感覺到褲子給浸濕了。他想把她扳起來，但她沉重得扳不動；她的肩膀抖動得非常厲害，即使是在這種情況下也使他感到

condition of this kind. Then she raised herself, tense but still trembling, and began a series of high-pitched, inward screams which alternated with the deep moans[2]. Both were quite loud. Her hair was in her eyes, her lips were drawn back, and her teeth chattered. Her face was wet, with saliva as well as tears. At last, as he began speaking her name, she threw herself violently backwards and sideways on to the bed. While she lay there with her arms spread out, writhing, she screamed half a dozen times, very loudly, then went on more quietly, moaning with every outward breath[3]. Dixon seized her wrists and shouted: "Margaret. Margaret." She looked at him with dilated eyes and began struggling, trying to free herself from him.

Kingsley Amis: Lucky Jim

很不正常。而後，她抬起身，樣子很緊張，仍舊打着顫，開始發出往裏吸氣的尖叫聲來，同時穿插着那種低沉的呻吟聲。尖叫聲和呻吟聲都很大。她頭髮掉到了眼睛裏，嘴唇向後拉着，牙齒直打哆嗦，臉上一把口水一把淚水。最後，當他開始呼喚她的名字的時候，她猛力朝後左右擺了擺，倒在牀上，兩手張開，胡亂翻滾，狂叫了六、七聲，然後又放低聲音繼續叫着，同時隨着向外呼氣呻吟着。狄克遜一把抓住她的手，叫道："瑪格麗特！瑪格麗特！"她張大眼睛望着他，掙扎起來，想擺脫他。

（英）金斯萊·艾米斯：《幸運的吉姆》

45　Unutterable Pain

In the afternoon of a certain summer's day, after Pearl
grew big enough to run about, she amused herself with
gathering handfuls of wild-flowers, and flinging them, one
by one, at her mother's bosom; dancing up and down, like a
little elf, whenever she hit the scarlet letter. Hester's first
motion had been to cover her bosom with her clasped hands.
But, whether from pride or resignation, or a feeling that her
penance might best be wrought out[1] by this unutterable pain,
she resisted the impulse, and sat erect, pale as death, looking
sadly into little Pearl's wild eyes. Still came the battery of
flowers, almost invariably hitting the mark, and covering the
mother's breasts with hurts for which she could find no balm
in this world, nor knew how to seek it in another. At last, her
shot being all expended, the child stood still and gazed at

1.　wrought out：原義 "精心製作"；這裏喻指抵償，耗盡。

四十五　痛苦難言

　　珠兒已經長大，可以跑來跑去了。一個夏日的午後，珠兒在玩耍，她採了一把把的野花，然後一枝一枝地往母親胸口上扔，每當她打中那紅字，就像個小精靈似的又蹦又跳。海絲特的第一個反應就是想緊握雙手捂住胸口。然而，不知是出於高傲還是無奈，或許她感到這種難言的痛苦是最好的贖罪方式，總之她剋制了這一衝動，挺直身子坐在那裏，面色死一樣的蒼白，傷心地盯着珠兒狂野的眼睛。野花接二連三地擲過來，幾乎無一例外地打在那個標記上，打得母親的胸口傷痕纍纍，使得她不僅在這個世界上找不到止痛膏，而且在另一個世界裏也無處尋覓。最後，珠兒的彈藥用盡了，她便一動不動地站着，盯着海絲

Hester, with that little, laughing image of a fiend peeping out — or whether it peeped or no, her mother so imagined it — from the unsearchable abyss of her black eyes.[2]

Nathaniel Hawthorne: The Scarlet Letter

---

2. the unsearchable abyss of her black eyes：珠兒是私生女，既是愛的結晶，也是罪孽的標誌；她是海絲特生活中的唯一希望，也是對她的折磨。海絲特多次產生一種幻覺，在女兒的眼睛裏，有一個她熟悉的、魔鬼似的面孔，或許那是她醜陋、矮小的丈夫，他曾聲稱要用一生的時間來復仇，因此他像幽靈一樣纏繞着海絲特。

特，從孩子那深不可測的黑眼睛裏，那個小小的、大笑的魔鬼形象也在窺視着她——或許根本沒有這回事，只不過是海絲特的想象罷了。

(美) 霍桑：《紅字》

46   Joint Affliction[1]

Elinor had not spirits to say more, and eager at all events to know what Willoughby[2] had written, hurried away to their room, where on opening the door she saw Marianne stretched on the bed, almost choked by grief, one letter in her hand and two or three others lying by her. Elinor drew near, but without saying a word; and seating herself on the bed, took her hand, kissed her affectionately several times, and then gave way to a burst of tears, which at first was scarcely less violent than Marianne's. The latter, though unable to speak, seemed to feel all the tenderness of this behaviour, and after some time thus spent in joint affliction[3], she put all the letters into Elinor's hands; and then covering her face with her handkerchief, almost screamed with agony. Elinor, who knew that such grief, shocking as it was to witness it, must have its course, watched by her till this excess of suffering had somewhat spent itself, and then turning eagerly to Willoughby's letter, read as follows: ...

Jane Austen: <u>Sense and Sensibility</u>

1.　本篇描寫姐姐為妹妹分擔失戀之苦的情景。

四十六　分擔痛苦

　　埃莉諾無心再說下去了，她急切地想知道威洛比來信的內容，便匆匆返回房間。一打開門，她便看到瑪麗安直挺挺地躺在牀上，幾乎泣不成聲，她手裏拿着一封信，身旁還放着兩、三封。埃麗諾走到她身邊，坐在牀沿，但一句話也沒有說，捧着她的手，情深地親吻了幾次，接着便失聲痛哭起來，一開始哭得跟瑪麗安一樣傷心。瑪麗安雖然一時說不出話來，但似乎完全感受到了姐姐的體貼與溫情。她們又這樣哭了一陣子，瑪麗安把幾封信都放在姐姐的手裏，然後用手帕捂住了臉，她痛苦得幾乎尖聲叫喊起來。埃麗諾明白，這樣的悲痛雖然看着很嚇人，但要有一段時間才能過去，因此她就在一旁照看着妹妹，直到她極度的悲傷漸漸平息下來，她才拿起威洛比的信，急切地看了起來……

　　　　　　　　　　　　（英）奧斯丁：《理智與情感》

2.　Willoughby：　威洛比，瑪麗安的心上人，他寫給她一封 "惡毒" 的信，令瑪麗安傷心不已。

3.　joint affliction：　共同的痛苦，指姐妹倆一起痛哭。

47 Grief

...desisting from their fruitless efforts[1], they seemed to abandon themselves to all the Oriental expressions of grief; the women making a piteous wailing, and tearing their long black hair, while the men seemed to rend their garments, and to sprinkle dust upon their heads.

Sir Walter Scott: Quentin Durward

---

1. efforts：指搶救死者的努力。

四十七　悲痛欲絕

　　他們看到一切努力都無濟於事，就以東方人的方式，渲洩着悲痛欲絕的心情。女人們號啕大哭，揪扯着自己長長的黑髮，那樣子令人哀憐；男人們撕扯着自己的衣服，還把塵土灑在頭上。

　　　　　　　　　　(英) 司各特：《昆丁·德沃得》

48   She Sank Helplessly on the Bed[1]

"Oh, God!" a terrible wail broke from her bosom.

She sank helplessly on the bed, her face buried in the pillows. But a moment later she sat up quickly, moved rapidly towards him, seized his hands and clasping them tightly, as though in a vice, in her thin fingers, stared motionlessly at him, her eyes glued to his face. With this last desperate look she tried to find some hope at least for herself and hold on to it. But there was no hope; there was no doubt whatever — it was true!

Dostoyevsky: Crime and Punishment

---

1. 索尼亞猜測到她的男友拉斯克尼科夫殺了人，驚恐萬分。本選段描寫了她絕望之中的動作、表情和言語。

四十八　絕望

　　"哦，天哪！"從她的胸腔裏發出了一聲可怕的哀號。

　　她一下子癱倒在牀上，臉埋在枕頭裏。可是不一會兒，她又猛地坐了起來，撲到他身邊，抓住他的雙手，她纖細的手指像老虎鉗一樣夾着他的手。她一動不動地、目不轉睛地盯着他。從這最後的、絕望的注視中，她試圖為自己尋找一絲希望，然後她會緊緊抓住不放。但是沒有希望了，毫無疑問，他真的殺了人。

　　　　　　　　（俄）陀思妥耶夫斯基：《罪與罰》

49　Fear[1]

That day there were two deaths; the following day three; then it jumped to eight. It was curious to see how we took it. The natives, for instance, fell into a condition of dumb, stolid fear. The captain — Oudouse, his name was, a Frenchman — became very nervous and voluble. He actually got the twitches. He was a large, fleshy man, weighing at least two hundred pounds, and he quickly became a faithful representation of a quivering jelly mountain of fat.

Jack London: "The Heathen"

1.　本篇描繪了由死亡引起的恐懼。在客船上，由於天花流行，乘客接二連三地死去，活着的人感到惶恐，有的害怕得説不出話，有的則渾身哆嗦，神經緊張到了極點。作者對此作了生動的刻劃。

四十九　恐懼

那天死了兩個人，第二天死了三個，然後一下子又死了八個。眾乘客對此的反應不一，這看來頗有幾分怪異。就說土人吧，他們嚇得目瞪口呆，一句話也說不出來。那個船長，一個叫烏都斯的法國人，則變得神經兮兮的，嘴裏嘀嘀咕咕說個不停，渾身抽搐不已。他是個大胖子，至少有兩百磅重，他哆嗦得厲害，很快就變成了一座活脫脫的顫抖着的脂肪山。

(美) 傑克・倫敦：“異教徒”

50 An Access of Terror

"A present from my master," said the groom.[1]

She was seized with[2] sudden apprehension. While feeling in her pocket for some money, she looked at the country fellow with a wild expression in her eye. He, for his part, gazed at her in astonishment, quite failing to understand why anyone should be so moved by so trivial a gift.

At last he left the room. Félicité[3] stayed where she was. Emma could stand the strain no longer, but ran into the parlour as though to arrange the apricots, turned the basket upside down, tore the leaves apart[4], found the letter, opened it, and then, as though a terrible fire were raging at her heels, fled in an access of terror to her room.

Charles[5] met her. She saw him. He said something to her. She did not hear but continued on her way upstairs, panting, distraught, like a drunken woman, still clutching

---

1. 禮物是愛瑪（包法利夫人）的情人羅道夫送來的。他經常把水果或野味放在籃子裏，把信藏在底層，讓僕人送來。在這封信裏，他提出要跟愛瑪分手。愛瑪似有此預感，因而表現出極度的惶恐。本篇是描寫這種驚慌失措情景的佳作。

2. was seized with： 被某種情緒所控制。

五十　驚惶失措

"這是我的主人給你的禮物。"僕人説。

她突然感到惶恐不安。她一邊在口袋裏摸錢，一邊望着那個鄉下人，眼裏帶着狂亂的神情。而他呢，則詫異地盯着她，不明白為甚麼有人會因這樣微薄的禮物而如此動情。

他終於走了。菲里西得還呆在那兒。愛瑪心裏很緊張，她再也忍受不了了，跑到客廳裏，好像要把杏子擺好。她把籃子翻倒過去，撥開葉子，找到了信，打開它，然後好像身後燃起了可怕的大火，驚惶失措地向自己的房間衝去。

查理碰上了她，她也看見他了。他對她説了些甚麼，她沒有聽到，接着往樓上跑，氣喘吁吁，慌慌張張，好像

---

3. Félicité：包法利家的女傭。

4. tear...apart：徹底搜查某處。

5. Charles：愛瑪的丈夫包法利先生。

the horrible sheet of paper which crackled in her fingers like metallic foil. On the second floor she stopped in front of the door leading to the attic. It was shut.

She tried to calm her nerves. She remembered the letter. She must read it to the end, but dared not. And where? Somebody would see her.

Here, she thought, I shall be safe. She pushed open the door and entered.

Gustave Flaubert: <u>Madame Bovary</u>

喝醉了酒，手裏仍緊緊攥着那張可怕的信紙，握得那信紙像金屬箔紙般，嘶啦嘶啦直響。她跑到三樓，在通向閣樓的門前停下來。門關着。

她試圖鎮靜下來，這才記起了那封信。她得讀完它，但她不敢。在哪裏看信呢？有人會發現她的。

這裏可以，她想，這裏是安全的。她推開門，走了進去。

(法) 福樓拜：《包法利夫人》

51　His Depths Remained Paralyzed

Clare perfomed the irrelevant act[1] of stirring the fire; the intelligence[2] had not even yet got to the bottom[3] of him. After stirring the embers he rose to his feet; all the force of her disclosure[4] had imparted itself now. His face had withered. In the strenuousness of his concentration he treadled fitfully on the floor. He could not, by any contrivance, think closely enough; that was the meaning of his vague movement[5]. When he spoke it was in the most inadequate, commonplace voice of the many varied tones she had heard from him.

"Tess!"

"Yes, dearest."

"Am I to believe this? From your manner I am to take it as true. O you cannot be out of your mind! You ought to be! Yet you are not ... My wife, my Tess — nothing in you warrants such a supposition as that?"

1.　irrelevant act：不合適、不相關的動作。苔絲向她的丈夫克萊爾表白了她失身的經過，克萊爾萬分震驚，一時間顯得茫然不知所措。本篇是對這種內心痛苦、表面不知所措的西方文化中紳士舉止和風度的細膩描寫。

2.　intelligence：消息，信息。這裏指苔絲敘述的事情。

五十一 茫然

克萊爾沒事找事地撥弄着爐火；他還沒有真正領會苔絲那段話的含義呢。撥完火，他站了起來；苔絲的話開始在他身上產生效力了。他的臉變得憔悴了。他一陣陣地在地上亂踩，努力地想把自己的思緒集中起來。他無論如何都不能集中精力思考，所以才作出這種茫然的舉動。他開口說話了，他說話的各種語調苔絲都聽過，而他這時的聲音最弱、最平板的一種。

"苔絲！"

"嗯，最親愛的！"

"難道我得相信這一切嗎？看你說話的樣子，我不該懷疑。哦，你不會是瘋了吧！你應該是瘋了！可你沒瘋……我的太太，我的苔絲，你身上沒有甚麼可以證明你是真的是瘋了嗎？"

---

3. bottom：內心深處。

4. disclosure：透露，即苔絲透露她失身的事情。

5. that was the meaning of his vague movement：他那茫然的動作（在地上亂踩）的含義是：他不能集中精神思考。that 代表它前面的那個句子。

"I am not out of my mind," she said.

"And yet —" He looked vacantly at her, to resume with dazed senses: "Why didn't you tell me before? Ah, yes, you would have told me, in a way — but I hindered you, I remember!"

These and other of his words were nothing but the perfunctory babble of the surface while the depths remained paralyzed[6]. He turned away, and bent over a chair.

Thomas Hardy: Tess of the d'Urbervilles

---

6. the perfunctory babble... paralyzed： 這裏 surface 和 depths 是相對照的。perfunctory：敷衍的。babble：胡言亂語。paralyzed：癱瘓了，麻木了。

“我沒有瘋，”她說。

“可是——”他茫然地看着她，又精神恍惚地接着說：“你為甚麼不早告訴我呢？啊，對了，你是想告訴我來着，但我阻止了你，我想起來了！”

這些話和其它的話只不過是表面上的敷衍罷了，他的內心深處仍然是一片麻木。他轉過身去，俯身靠在一把椅子上。

(英) 哈代：《德伯家的苔絲》

52 A Peculiar Expression[1]

Jim stopped inside the door, as immovable as a setter at the scent of quail. His eyes were fixed upon Della, and there was an expression in them that she could not read, and it terrified her. It was not anger, nor surprise, nor disapproval, nor horror, nor any of the sentiments that she had been prepared for. He simply stared at her fixedly with that peculiar expression on his face.

O. Henry: "The Gift of the Magi"

---

1. 聖誕前夕，吉姆賣掉了他最心愛的金錶，給妻子德拉買了一套精美的髮梳。可他回到家裏，卻驚異地發現，妻子已將秀髮賣掉，給他換了一條錶鏈。此段即是對吉姆臉上驚異古怪表情的生動描寫。

五十二　驚呆

　　他一進門就停住了，就像獵犬嗅到鵪鶉，一動也不動。他兩眼盯住德拉，眼中神情令德拉大惑不解，簡直嚇壞了她。那神情不是憤怒，不是驚奇，不是反對，不是恐懼，也不是她所能設想的任何情緒。他只是呆呆地盯着她，臉上帶着那古怪的表情。

　　　　　　　　　　　（美）歐·亨利：《賢士的禮物》

53   He Could Not Help Blushing[1]

"I suppose you've got talipes equinus[2]?" he said, turning suddenly to Philip.

"Yes."

Philip felt the eyes of his fellow-students rest on him, and he cursed himself because he could not help blushing. He felt the sweat start up in the palms of his hands....

"You don't mind taking off your sock for a moment, Carey?"

Philip felt a shudder pass through him. He had an impulse to tell the surgeon to go to hell, but he had not the courage to make a scene[3]. He feared his brutal ridicule. He forced himself to appear indifferent.

"Not at all," he said.

---

1. 菲利普來到外科門診,在雅各布醫生的指導下實習。一天,雅各布大談特談跛足的類型和構造,並要菲利普當眾裸露他的跛足,令他窘迫不已。

2. talipes equinus : 馬蹄形的畸形足。talipes:(醫學用語)畸形足。equinus:(拉丁語)馬的。

3. make a scene : 當眾吵鬧,發脾氣。

五十三　窘迫

　　"我想你的跛足是馬蹄形的吧？"外科醫生雅各布突然轉向菲利普問道。

　　"是的。"

　　菲利普感覺到同學們的眼睛都在注視着他，他不由得滿臉通紅，為此，他暗暗地責罵自己。他的手掌上滲出了汗水。……

　　"你把襪子脫下來一會兒，不介意吧，凱里？"

　　菲利普覺得渾身一顫。一時衝動之下，他巴不得叫雅各布去見鬼。但是他沒有勇氣發脾氣，他害怕受到無情的嘲弄，所以強迫自己擺出滿不在乎的樣子。

　　"當然不介意，"他說。

He sat down and unlaced his boot. His fingers were trembling, and he thought he should never untie the knot. He remembered how they had forced him at school to show his foot and the misery which had eaten into his soul[4].

W. Somerset Maugham: Of Human Bondage

---

4. the misery that had eaten into his soul： 字面意義為 "吞噬腐蝕他靈魂的痛楚"。

他坐下來，開始解靴子帶。他的手指在發抖，他覺得自己根本不該解開鞋帶。他回憶起上學的時候同學們強迫他裸露跛足情景，回憶起那種刻骨銘心的痛楚。

　　　　　　　　　（英）毛姆：《人性的枷鎖》

54　Stage-fright[1]

... he hurried out and into the Staff Cloakroom[2]. Stage-fright was upon him now; his hands were cold and damp, his legs felt like flaccid rubber tubes filled with fine sand, he had difficulty in controlling his breathing. While he was using the lavatory, he began making his Evelyn Waugh[3] face, then abandoned it in favour of one more savage than any he normally used. Gripping his tongue between his teeth, he made his cheeks expand into little hemispherical balloons; he forced his upper lip downwards into an idiotic pout; he protruded his chin like the blade of a shovel. Throughout, he alternately dilated and crossed his eyes.

Kingsley Amis: Lucky Jim

---

1. 狄克遜是某大學的合同講師，他想作一次出色的演講，以保住自己的飯碗。出場前，他特別緊張，做出種種怪相給自己打氣。這一段的描寫維妙維肖，筆調幽默諷刺。

2. Cloakroom：衣帽間；也是廁所的委婉語。

3. Evelyn Waugh (1903-66)：英國小說家，擅長諷刺英國上流社會的流弊及禮儀。

五十四　怯場

　　……他匆忙地走了出去，來到教職員的洗手間裏。這時，他感到怯場了；他的手掌又冷又濕，兩條腿就像灌滿細沙的橡膠管一樣軟弱無力，呼吸也困難。他一面如廁，一面使出一副幽默小説家伊夫林・沃式的怪相，接着又放棄這副怪相，轉換出一副比平時更加粗魯的鬼臉。他先把舌頭咬在兩排牙齒中間，使兩頰隆起，變成兩個半圓形的小氣球；然後他使勁讓上唇往下唇壓，壓出一個白癡般的噘嘴；接着，他又把下巴朝外翹起，翹得像把鐵鏟一樣。從頭至尾，他還時而鼓起眼睛，時而像長着鬥雞眼一樣地轉動眼珠。

　　　　　（英）金斯萊・艾米斯：《幸運的吉姆》

55 Leapt upon the Gold Dressing Case[1]

Just as he came up the stairs to his wife's room with catlike tread (he happened to have taken the master key with him) Eugenie was laying the beautiful gold dressing case[2] on her mother's bed. In the old man's absence, the two of them were indulging in the pleasure of looking for Charles' features in the portrait of his mother.

"It's his forehead and his mouth exactly!" Eugenie was saying just as the vintner opened the door.

Seeing her husband's expression as he looked at the gold, Mme. Grandet cried,

"God have mercy upon us!"

The old man leapt upon the gold dressing case the way a tiger would pounce on a sleeping child.

"What's this? What's this?" he asked, picking up the treasure and going over to the window. "Gold! Solid gold[3]! And a lot of it," he cried. "Why, it must weigh two pounds!

---

1. 本篇寫的是老葡萄酒商葛朗台的貪婪行為。英語原文中的 he, the vintner, the old man, the cooper 都是指這同一人，但根據漢語的表達習慣，在一篇並不太長的文字裏，一般不會用許多不同的名稱來指同一人，因此在翻譯中有必要做出調整，即把"老葡萄商"調到前面指明"他"是誰，把"老箍桶匠"(cooper)刪去，以免誤解為另一人。

五十五　貪婪

　　老葡萄酒商像貓一樣躡手躡腳地走上樓梯，來到他太太的房間（他碰巧拿着萬能鑰匙），歐也妮正把那隻漂亮的鑲金的梳妝盒放到母親的牀上。趁老頭不在，母女倆正滿心歡喜地從查理母親的肖像中尋找他的特徵。

　　"這就是他的額頭和嘴呀！"歐也妮說這話的時候，老葡萄酒商正好打開了門。

　　看到丈夫發現金子時的表情，葛朗台夫人叫了起來：

　　"上帝呀，救救我們！"

　　老頭身子一躍，撲向鑲金的梳妝盒，就像一頭老虎撲向酣睡的嬰兒。

　　"這是甚麼？這是甚麼？"他問，抓起寶盒，走到窗邊。"金子！真金！還不少呢，"他喊道。"哇，足有兩

---

2. dressing case：梳妝盒。這個梳妝盒是歐也妮的堂弟和戀人查理出國前託付給她的，裏面裝有他父母的畫像。

3. solid gold：純金。solid：純質的。

Ha! So Charles gave this to you in exchange for your pretty coins, did he? Why didn't you tell me? You made a good little bargain there, my sweet! You are a true daughter of mine, I can see."

Eugenie was trembling in every limb.

"This does belong to Charles, doesn't it?" pursued the old man.

"Yes, father. It's not mine. This case is a sacred trust."

"Tch, tch, tch, tch! He took away your fortune, you can use this to replace it."

"Father! ..."

In order to take out his knife and pry off some of the gold, the old man was obliged to rest the case on a chair for a moment. Eugenie rushed forward to retrieve it, but the cooper, who had one eye on his daughter and the other on the little case, thrust out his arm and pushed her away so violently that she fell back onto her mother's bed.

"Sir!" cried the mother, raising herself from her pillow.

Grandet had his knife in hand and was preparing to pry off the gold.

Honoré de Balzac: <u>Eugénie Grandet</u>

磅重。哈！查理用這個換了你那些美麗的金幣，是不是？你為甚麼不告訴我？這很合算，小乖乖！你真是我的好女兒，我看得出來。"

歐也妮四肢發抖。

"這個真是查理的，對嗎？"老頭逼問了一句。

"是的，父親。這不是我的。這盒子是人家鄭重地託我保管的。"

"唔，唔，唔，唔！他拿走了你的財產，你可以用這個來代替。"

"父親！"

老頭想拿出刀子，撬下一些金子來，就只好先把盒子放在椅子上。歐也妮衝上去想搶回來，但是老頭一隻眼睛盯着女兒，另一隻眼睛盯着盒子，他胳膊一甩，推開女兒，由於用力過猛，歐也妮一下子仰倒在母親的牀上。

"老爺！"母親喊着，從枕頭上抬起身。

葛朗台手拿刀子，準備撬金子。

(法) 巴爾扎克：《歐也妮‧葛朗台》

56　Lousy with Perverts

After he left, I looked out the window for a while, with my coat on and all[1]. I didn't have anything else to do. You'd be surprised what was going on on the other side of the hotel. They didn't even bother to pull their shades down. I saw one guy, a gray-haired, very distinguished-looking guy with only his shorts on, do something you wouldn't believe me if I told you. First he put his suitcase on the bed. Then he took out all these women's clothes, and put them on. Real women's clothes — silk stockings, high-heeled shoes, brassière, and one of those corsets with the straps hanging down and all. Then he put on this very tight black evening dress. I swear to God. Then he started walking up and down the room, taking these very small steps, the way a woman does, and smoking a cigarette and looking at himself in the mirror. He was all alone, too. Unless somebody was in the bathroom — I couldn't see that much. Then, in the window almost right over his, I saw a man and a woman squirting water out of

---

1.　and all：以及其他一切。

五十六　心理變態

　　他走了以後，我沒脫大衣或甚麼，向窗外望了一會兒。我沒有其他事情可做。酒店另一面所發生的事情，會令你大吃一驚。他們甚至懶得將窗簾放下來。我看到一個頭髮花白、模樣出眾的男人，只穿着一條短褲，他的所做所為，我說出來你會難以相信。他先把手提箱放在牀上，然後拿出來許多女人的衣服，一件一件穿上。那是些名副其實的女人的衣服——長統絲襪、高跟鞋、胸罩和有兩條吊帶的緊身胸衣。然後他又穿上了一件緊身的黑色晚禮服。我可以對天發誓。接着他在房間裏走來走去，像女人那樣邁着碎步，嘴裏還叼着煙，對着鏡子欣賞自己。他是單獨一人，除非浴室裏有人——我看不到。後來，大約在這扇窗戶的正上方，我又看到一男一女嘴裏含着水向對方

their mouths at each other. It probably was highballs[2], not water, but I couldn't see what they had in their glasses. Anyway, first he'd take a swallow and squirt it all over her, then she did it to him — they took turns, for God's sake. You should've seen them. They were in hysterics the whole time, like it was the funniest thing that ever happened. I'm not kidding, the hotel was lousy with[3] perverts.

J.D. Salinger: <u>The Catcher in the Rye</u>

---

2. highballs：高杯酒。用威士忌或白蘭地等烈酒攙水或汽水加冰塊製成的飲料，盛在高腳杯內飲用。

3. lousy with：充滿着 (俗語貶義)。

身上噴射。也許不是水，是高杯酒，我看不到他們杯子裏的東西。反正是他先喝了一口，噴了她一身，跟着她也照樣噴他——他們輪流着噴來噴去，老天爺呀。你真該見見他們。他們一直都在發歇斯底里，彷彿這是世界上最有趣的事情。我不是在開玩笑，這家酒店裏住滿了心理變態的人。

（美）塞林格：《麥田裏的守望者》

57 Locked in an Embrace[1]

In her eagerness she rose, and supported herself on the arm of the chair. At that earnest appeal, he turned to her, looking absolutely desperate. His eyes wide, and wet, at last, flashed fiercely on her; his breast heaved convulsively. An instant they held asunder; and then how they met I hardly saw, but Catherine made a spring, and he caught her, and they were locked in an embrace from which I thought my mistress would never be released alive. In fact, to my eyes, she seemed directly insensible. He flung himself into the nearest seat, and on my approaching hurriedly to ascertain if she had fainted, he gnashed at me, and foamed[2] like a mad dog, and gathered her to him with greedy jealousy. I did not feel as if I were in the company of a creature of my own species; it appeared that he would not understand, though I spoke to him; so, I stood off, and held my tongue, in great perplexity.

A movement of Catherine's relieved me a little presently: she put up her hand to clasp his neck, and bring her cheek to his, as he held her: while he, in return, covering her with frantic caresses,...

Emily Brontë: Wuthering Heights

五十七　擁抱

　　她急切地站起來，雙手撐在椅子的扶手上。受到她真切的懇求，他轉向她，露出不顧一切的神情。他的眼睛睜得大大的，含着淚水，終於向她發出熱切的光芒，。他的胸膛也急劇地起伏着。剎那間，他們分開了；然後，我沒有看清楚他們是怎麼抱在一起的，只看到凱瑟琳向前一躍，他就摟住了她。他們緊緊地擁抱着，我想我的女主人絕不會被活着放開了。事實上，據我看，她似乎即刻就失去了知覺。他跌坐到最近的椅子上，我急忙走向前看看她是否暈過去了，他就對我咬牙切齒，瘋狗般地發怒，把她抱緊，一副又貪婪又嫉妒的樣子。我真感到我面對的不是一個與我同類的動物。看來我說甚麼他也不會明白的。所以我困惑地站到一旁，默不作聲。

　　凱瑟琳動了一下，我馬上鬆了一口氣。他摟着她，她伸手緊緊抱住他的脖子，貼近他的臉，他回報給她的是瘋狂的愛撫，⋯⋯

　　　　　　　　（英）艾米莉·勃朗特：《呼嘯山莊》

1.　本篇以一個女傭的口吻，描述了一對舊日情人重逢時的感人場面。
2.　foamed：大怒，（發怒時）唾沫四濺。

58   An Experiment Kiss[1]

One evening, when, at bedtime, his sisters and I stood round him, bidding him goodnight, he kissed each of them, as was his custom; and, as was equally his custom, he gave me his hand. Diana, who chanced to be in a frolicsome humour[1] (she was not painfully controlled by his will; for hers, in another way, was as strong), exclaimed:

"St John! You used to call Jane your third sister, but you don't treat her as such: you should kiss her too."

She pushed me towards him. I thought Diana very provoking, and felt uncomfortably confused; and while I was thus thinking and feeling, St John bent his head; his Greek face[2] was brought to a level with mine, his eyes questioned my eyes piercingly — he kissed me. There are no such things as marble kisses or ice kisses, or I should say my ecclesiastical cousin's salute[3] belonged to one of these classes; but there may be experiment kisses, and his was an experiment kiss. When given, he viewed me to learn the result; it was not

---

1. humour：心情，心境。
2. his Greek face：他的希臘型的臉，意指古典型的臉。
3. salute：致意，這裏指聖約翰的吻。

154

五十八　試吻

　　一天晚上，在就寢之前，他的兩個妹妹和我都站在他身旁跟他道晚安，他照例一一吻了她們，然後又照例把手伸給我。黛安娜碰巧心情愉快，（她可不會難為自己，為他的意志所左右，因為她的意志也一樣堅強，不過方式不同），她嚷道：

　　"聖約翰！你說過簡是你的三妹，可你沒有這樣待她，你也應該吻吻她。"

　　她把我推到他面前。我覺得黛安娜簡直無事生非，我感到又彆扭又尷尬。正當我抱着這樣的心情和想法的時候，聖約翰低下了頭，他那古典型的臉低到跟我的臉一般平，他以銳利的目光探視着我的眼睛——他吻了我。世上沒有石頭吻或者冰吻那樣的東西，不然的話，我就要說我這位教士表哥的吻就是屬於這一類的。不過可能會有試驗性的親吻吧，那他的吻就是這一種了。吻完以後，他打量着我，看看結果如何。結果並不明顯，我敢肯定我沒有臉

striking: I am sure I did not blush; perhaps I might have turned a little pale, for I felt as if this kiss were a seal affixed to my fetters[4]. He never omitted the ceremony afterwards, and the gravity and quiescence with which I underwent it, seemed to invest it for him with a certain charm.

Charlotte Brontë: <u>Jane Eyre</u>

---

4. a seal affixed to my fetters：聖約翰有些冷漠和專制，對簡的控制過多。簡覺得表哥的吻對她來説也是一種約束和負擔。

紅，也許我變得稍稍蒼白了一點，因為我覺得這一吻就彷彿是加在我的鐐銬上的封鉛似的。從此以後，他就沒有忽略過這個禮節，而我被吻的時候總是一本正經，不動聲色，這似乎倒使他感到頗為有趣。

(英) 夏洛蒂·勃朗特：《簡·愛》

59　A Huge Warm Pole of Desire

He drew her closer, till he felt her breath coming full in his face. The wind swept against the windowpane and the building, whining, then whispered out into silence. He turned from his back and lay face to face with her, on his side. He kissed her; her lips were cold. He kept kissing her until her lips grew warm and soft. A huge warm pole of desire rose in him, insistent and demanding; he let his hand slide from her shoulder to her breasts, feeling one, then the other; he slipped his other arm beneath her head, kissing her again, hard and long.

"Please, Bigger..."

...

Her voice came to him now from out of a deep, far-away silence and he paid her no heed. The loud demand of the tensity of his own body was a voice that drowned out hers. In the cold darkness of the room it seemed that he was on some vast turning wheel that made him want to turn faster and faster; that in turning faster he would get warmth and sleep and be rid of his tense fatigue. He was conscious of nothing now but her and what he wanted. He flung the cover back, ignoring the cold, and not knowing that he did it.

五十九　慾火

　　他把她摟得更緊了，直到他感覺得她的氣息直撲到他的臉上。風拍打着窗玻璃和樓房，嗚咽着，低語着，最後寂靜一片。他翻了個身，側躺着，和她面對面。他吻她，她的嘴唇冷冷的。他不斷地吻着她，直到她的嘴唇變得溫暖而柔軟。一大團熱烘烘的慾火從他的體內升起，那麼執着，那麼迫切；他的手從她的肩膀滑落到她的胸脯上，摸到一個乳房，然後又摸另一個；他的另一隻手臂伸到她的頭下面，他又吻她，使勁地、長時間的吻着。

　　"求求你，比格……"

　　……

　　現在她的聲音彷彿從很深很遠的寂靜中向他飄來，他毫不理會。他自己那繃緊的身體內的大聲需求，把她的聲音淹沒了。在冰冷黑暗的房間裏，他似乎置身於一個巨大的、旋轉的輪子上，他只想轉得快一些，更快一些；飛速的旋轉中，他會變得溫暖，安然入睡，擺脫掉緊張與疲憊。他現在的意識中，只有她和他的慾望。他把被子掀開，感覺不到寒冷，他意識不到自己在做甚麼。貝西的手

Bessie's hands were on his chest, her fingers spreading protestingly open, pushing him away. He heard her give a soft moan that seemed not to end even when she breathed in or out; a moan which he heard, too, from far away and without heeding. He had to now. Imperiously driven, he rode roughshod over[1] her whimpering protests, feeling acutely sorry for her as he galloped a frenzied horse down a steep hill in the face of a resisting wind, *don't don't don't Bigger*. And then the wind became so strong that it lifted him high into the dark air, turning him, twisting him, hurling him; faintly, over the wind's howl, he heard: *don't Bigger don't don't*. At a moment he could not remember, he had fallen; and now he lay, spent, his lips parted.

Richard Wright: <u>Native Son</u>

1.　rode roughshod over：對……不予理睬或同情，欺凌或粗暴地對待。

頂在他的胸口上，手指抗議似地分開，想把他推走。他聽到她輕輕地呻吟着，甚至在她呼氣、吸氣的時候，這聲呻吟也沒有中斷；這聲呻吟也好像從很遠的地方傳來，他不加理會。他現在控制不住自己了。在迫切的慾望的驅使下，他全然不顧她哼哼唧唧的抗議，好像騎在一匹瘋狂的馬上，頂着逆風，順着陡峭的山坡飛馳而下，風中傳來她的聲音，"不要不要不要，比格"，他感到很對不起她。接着風颳得很猛，竟把他高高舉到黑暗的空中，旋轉着他，扭動着他，猛推着他；在狂風的怒吼聲中，他依稀地聽到"不要，比格，不要不要"。不知在甚麼時候，他已經掉下來了，現在他躺在那兒，雙唇張開，精疲力盡。

（美）理查·賴特：《土生子》

60　Be My Wife[1]

"I say agin[2], I want you," Sir Pitt said, thumping the table. "I can't git on[3] without you. I didn't see what it was till you went away. The house all goes wrong. It's not the same place. All my accounts has got muddled agin. You must come back. Do come back. Dear Becky[4], do come."

"Come — as what, sir?" Rebecca gasped out.

"Come as Lady Crawley, if you like," the baronet said, grasping his crape[5] hat. "There! Will that zatusfy[6] you? Come back and be my wife. Your vit vor't.[7] Birth be hanged.[8] Your as good a lady as ever I see. You've got more brains in your little vinger[9] than any baronet's wife in the county. Will you come? Yes or no?"

"Oh, Sir Pitt!" Rebecca said, very much moved.

---

1. 皮特爵士認為他的家庭教師麗貝卡會得到一筆遺產，便不顧自己的貴族身份向她求婚。在這裏作者諷刺了資產階級的婚姻關係──為錢結婚。皮特爵士講話有漢普郡（Hampshire）方言的特點，如：將開頭的 f 唸成 v，s 唸成 z 等。

2. agin：＝ again

3. git on：＝ get on　生活。

4. Becky：Rebecca 的昵稱

六十　求婚

　　"我再説一遍，我要你，"皮特爵士拍着桌子喊道，"沒有你我過不下去。你離開之後我才明白過來。家裏亂七八糟的，完全變了樣，我所有的賬目又都變成糊塗賬了。你一定得回來，求求你，回來吧！親愛的貝基，回來吧！"

　　"回來——做甚麼呢？"麗貝卡呼吸急促地問。

　　"願意的話，就回來做克勞萊夫人。"男爵抓着他那纏着黑紗的帽子説，"怎麼樣！滿意了嗎？回來做我的夫人吧。你配得上我。去他的甚麼門第吧！你是我見到的最像樣的淑女。你聰明過人，郡裏所有的男爵夫人都比不上你。怎麼樣？回來還是不回來？"

　　"哦，皮特爵士！"麗貝卡喊到，她感動極了。

---

5. crape：(佩在袖子或帽子上以表示哀悼的)黑紗。皮特爵士的夫人剛剛去世，他正在辦理喪事。

6. zatusfy：＝ satisfy

7. Your vit vor't：＝ You're fit for it，你配得上做我的妻子。

8. Birth be hanged：birth 指出身，血統，門第。be hanged 本義"吊死"；這裏是粗俗語，表示"去他的"。

9. vinger：＝ finger

"Say yes, Becky," Sir Pitt continued. "I'm an old man, but a good'n[10]. I'm good for twenty years. I'll make you happy, zee[11] if I don't. You shall do what you like; spend what you like; and 'av[12] it all your own way. I'll make you a zettlement[13]. I'll do everything reglar[14]. Look year[15]!" and the old man fell down on his knees and leered at her like a satyr[16].

Rebecca started back, a picture of consternation. In the course of this history we have never seen her lose her presence of mind; but she did now, and wept some of the most genuine tears that ever fell from her eyes.

"Oh, Sir Pitt!" she said. "Oh, sir — I — I'm *married already.*"

W.M. Thackeray: Vanity Fair

---

10. a good'n：= a good one，指身體健康的人。

11. zee：= see

12. 'av = have

13. zettlement：= settlement，財產。

“答應吧，貝基，”皮特爵士接着説，“我上了年紀，但身體還很好。還可以好好活上二十年。我會讓你開心的，你看看我能不能做到。你願意做甚麼都行，花多少錢都可以；可以隨心所欲。我會給你一筆財產。我幹甚麼都會規規矩矩的。你瞧！”接着老頭兒雙膝跪下，色迷迷地斜睨着她。

　　麗貝卡驚得直往後退，一副驚慌失措的樣子。故事講到這裏以前，她一直都表現得鎮定自若，可現在她慌了，掉下淚來，這大概是她有生以來最真誠的幾滴眼淚。

　　“哦，皮特爵士！”她説，“哦，皮特爵士——我——我已經結過婚了。”

　　　　　　　　　　　　　　（英）薩克雷：《名利場》

---

14. reglar ＝ regular
15. look year：＝ look here
16. satyr：希臘神話裏的森林的神，代表好色的人。

61 Honeymoon

They took an afternoon train for New York, which required five hours to reach. When they were finally alone in the Astor House, New York, after hours of make believe[1] and public pretense of indifference, he gathered her in his arms.

"Oh, it's delicious," he exclaimed, "to have you all to myself[2]."

She met his eagerness with that smiling, tantalizing passivity which he had so much admired but which this time was tinged strongly with[3] a communicated desire. He thought he should never have enough of her, her beautiful face, her lovely arms, her smooth, lymphatic body. They were like two children, billing and cooing[4], driving, dining, seeing the sights.

Theodore Dreiser: The Financier

---

1. make believe：假裝，假扮。這是個動詞短語，在此做名詞用。
2. to have you all to myself：也可譯為 "讓你完全屬於我。"
3. tinged... with：帶有……痕迹。

六十一　蜜月

　　他們乘下午的火車去紐約，要五個小時才能到達。這幾個小時當中，他們只得假扮正經，在眾人面前裝得彼此漠不關心。當他們終於到達紐約阿斯特酒店的時候，他一把摟住了她。

　　"哦，這多好！"他喊道，"我能單獨和你在一起。"

　　她微笑着接受了他熱烈的擁抱，順從中略帶挑逗。這種姿態是他一向十分讚賞的，不過這一回，她明顯有着與他相同的欲望。他覺得她的美是他永遠享用不夠的：她漂亮的面孔、可愛的手臂、光滑柔美的身體。他們就像兩個孩子，相互愛撫着，親昵地交談着，驅車遊玩，盡情吃喝，遊覽名勝。

（美）德萊塞：《金融家》

---

4. billing and cooing：bill 原指鴿子接嘴；coo 指鴿子鴣鴣之聲；喻指戀人談情時親吻及喁喁細語的情景。

62　He Put out His Hand and Took Hers[1]

Finally, while the echoes of the last stroke of ten were still hanging in the air, he put out his hand and took Madame de Rênal's; she withdrew it immediately. Julien, not too clearly aware of what he was doing, seized it again. Although he himself was deeply moved, he was struck by the icy coldness of the hand he was holding. He squeezed it with convulsive force; she made a final effort to draw it away from him, but finally it remained in his grasp.

Henri Beyle Stendhal: The Red and the Black

1.　在夜幕降臨的花園裏，于連（Julien）終於鼓足勇氣，做出了他計劃已久的舉動 —— 與他暗戀的得瑞那夫人（Madame de Rênal's）親近。

六十二　偷情

　　終於，當十點鐘聲的最後一響餘音未絕時，于連伸出了手，抓住了得瑞那夫人的玉手，她馬上縮了回去。于連又一次抓住了她的手，他並不大清楚自己在做甚麼。儘管他已是心神搖蕩，他捉住的那隻冰冷的手還是令他砰然心動。他衝動地緊緊揑着那隻玉手；得瑞那夫人最後掙扎了一下，想把手抽回去，但最後還是聽之任之了。

　　　　　　　　　　　(法) 斯丹達爾：《紅與黑》

63 A Railway Journey[1]

She was gay, like a sweetheart. She stood in front of the ticket-office at Bestwood, and Paul watched her take from her purse the money for the tickets. As he saw her hands in their old black kid gloves getting the silver out of the worn purse, his heart contracted with pain[2] of love of her.

She was quite excited, and quite gay. He suffered because she *would* talk aloud in the presence of other travellers.

"Now look at that silly cow!" she said, "careering round as if it thought it was a circus."

"It's most likely a botfly," he said very low.

"A what?" she asked brightly and unashamed.

They thought a while. He was sensible all the time of having her opposite him. Suddenly their eyes met, and she smiled to him — a rare, intimate smile, beautiful with brightness and love. Then each looked out of the window.

---

1. 本篇通過莫雷爾夫人和兒子保羅一同旅行時的動作、表情、對話和心理活動，表現出母子之間奧狄浦斯式 (Oedipus) 戀母的感情。
2. 保羅是個很敏感的孩子，母親的貧窮和她在公共場合舉止言行的不妥都令他感到痛苦。

六十三　母子同行

　　她快樂得像個情人。她站在白斯伍得村的售票處前，從錢包裏掏錢買票，保羅在一旁注視着她。她手上帶着黑色的、小山羊皮製的舊手套，從破舊的錢包裏拿出銀幣，看到這些，保羅的心被一陣愛的痛苦扭緊了。

　　她很興奮，很快樂。他的心裏卻很難受，因為她總是在其他旅客面前大聲地講話。

　　“看那頭蠢牛！”她說，“繞着圈子跑來跑去，好像覺得自己在作馬戲表演。”

　　“可能是因為有一隻馬蠅在牠頭上飛，”他很小聲地說。

　　“一隻甚麼？”她興高采烈地問，絲毫未感到不好意思。

　　他們沉思了片刻。他每時每刻都意識到她就在對面。忽然間，他們的目光相遇了，她對他一笑，那是一種不常見、親昵、動人的微笑，流露出歡欣和愛意。隨後，他們將視綫移到窗外。

The sixteen slow miles of railway journey passed. The mother and son walked down Station Street, feeling the excitement of lovers having an adventure together.

D.H. Lawrence: <u>Sons and Lovers</u>

火車緩緩地走了十六英里。下了火車，母子倆走在車站街上。他們很興奮，就像一對情侶在結伴冒險。

　　　　　　　(英) 勞倫斯：《兒子與情人》

64 Her Mother Loved Her More Every Day

... Her mother loved her[1] more every day. She hugged her, kissed her, played with her, washed her and dressed her every minute she could spare. She was almost wild with joy and never stopped thanking God for her. Those pink little feet, especially, were an endless wonder to her. She was always kissing them and was always amazed at how tiny they were. She would spend whole hours putting the little shoes on them and taking them off again.

Victor Hugo: <u>The Hunchback of Notre Dame</u>

---

1. her：指襁褓之中的愛斯梅拉達。

六十四　舐犢之情

　　媽媽對女兒的愛與日俱增。她一有空閒就抱着她，親吻她，逗她玩兒，給她洗澡、穿衣服。有了女兒，她欣喜若狂，幾乎每時每刻都在感激上帝的恩賜。尤其對女兒那雙粉紅色的小腳，她愛不釋手，不停地親吻着，它們玲瓏精緻，令她讚嘆不已。她給孩子穿上小鞋，再脫下來，她這樣穿穿脫脫數小時，樂此不疲。

　　　　　　　　　　(法）雨果：《鐘樓駝俠》

65 The Child Began to Cry Loudly

Again the infant whimpered and twisted in its sleep, its lips drawn back showing the gums: its knees pressed closely to its body, the little fists clenched, and face flushed. Then after a few seconds it became placid: the mouth resumed its usual shape; the limbs relaxed and the child slumbered peacefully.

...

The child in the cradle — who had been twisting and turning restlessly all this time — now began to cry loudly. The mother took it from the cradle and began to hush and soothe it, walking about the room and rocking it in her arms. The child, however, continued to scream, so she sat down to nurse it: for a little while the infant refused to drink, struggling and kicking in its mother's arms, then for a few minutes it was quiet, taking the milk in a half-hearted, fretful way. Then it again began to scream and twist and struggle.

Robert Tressell: The Ragged Trousered Philanthropist

六十五 哭鬧

嬰兒又在睡夢中嗚咽、抽搐起來，他嘴唇蜷縮，露出牙牀；膝蓋緊貼着身體，小拳頭緊握着，小臉紅紅的。過了一會兒，他平靜下來了：小嘴恢復了正常的形狀，四肢放鬆，安然入睡了。

……

一直在搖籃裏翻來覆去地抽搐着的孩子，這會兒開始大聲地哭叫。媽媽把他從搖籃裏抱出來，哄着、撫慰着他，邊在屋裏踱步，邊把他搖來搖去。可是孩子仍然尖聲地哭着，她只好坐下來給他餵奶：開頭一陣，孩子不肯吃，在媽媽懷裏掙扎着，亂踢亂蹬，幾分鐘之後才不鬧了，愛吃不吃地煩躁地吮着。過了一會兒，他又開始了尖叫、抽搐和掙扎。

（英）羅伯特·特雷塞爾：《穿破褲子的慈善家》

66　You Must Come and Be Undressed[1]

"You must come and be undressed," he said, in a quiet voice that was thin with anger.

And he reached his hand and grasped her. He felt her body catch in a convulsive sob. But he too was blind, and intent, irritated into mechanical action. He began to unfasten her little apron. She would have shrunk from him, but could not. So her small body remained in his grasp, while he fumbled at the little buttons and tapes, unthinking, intent, unaware of anything but the irritation of her. Her body was held taut and resistant, he pushed off the little dress and the petticoats, revealing the white arms. She kept stiff, overpowered, violated, he went on with his task. And all the while she sobbed, choking:

"I want my mother."

...

"Where is her nightie?" he asked.

---

1. 布朗溫的妻子因臨產的陣痛而不停地呻吟，他心亂如麻。本篇通過他
　　給女兒安娜換衣服時的一系列的動作和聲音，描繪出他焦慮不安的心
　　情。

六十六　更換衣服

　　"你過來，把衣服脱了，"布朗温説，慍怒使他的聲音變得薄弱。

　　他伸出手去一把抓住她，感覺到她的身體因嗚咽而抽搐。但他被激怒了，失去了理智，一意孤行、機械地行動起來。他開始解她的小圍裙。她想縮開，但又掙脱不來。她小小的身體被他抓在手裏，他摸索着解開她的小扣子、小帶子。他腦子裏一片空白，全神貫注；除了她的煩厭，其他甚麼也不想。小姑娘渾身緊張，不停地反抗，他扯下她的小裙子和襯裙，她白白的胳膊露了出來。她渾身僵硬，被他粗暴的舉動鎮住了。他繼續給她脱衣服，而她一直上氣不接下氣地啜泣着：

　　"我要媽媽。"

　　……

　　"她的睡衣呢？"他問。

Tilly brought it, and he put it on her. Anna did not move her limbs to his desire. He had to push them into place.... He lifted one foot after the other, pulled off slippers and socks. She was ready.

D.H. Lawrence: *The Rainbow*

蒂莉拿來睡衣，他給她穿上。安娜的四肢不聽他的使喚。他只好用力地去拉去拽。……他提起她的一隻腳，然後另一隻腳，脫下了她的拖鞋和襪子。她換好衣服了。

（英）勞倫斯《彩虹》

67　She Was Silent[1]

Holding the child on one arm, he set about preparing the food for the cows, filling a pan with chopped hay and brewer's grains and a little meal. The child, all wonder, watched what he did. A new being was created in her for the new conditions. Sometimes, a little spasm, eddying from the bygone storm of sobbing, shook her small body. Her eyes were wide and wondering, pathetic. She was silent, quite still[2].

In a sort of dream, his heart sunk to the bottom, leaving the surface of him still, quite still, he rose with the panful of food, carefully balancing the child on one arm, the pan in the other hand. The silky fringe of the shawl[3] swayed softly, grains and hay trickled to the floor; he went along a dimly-lit passage behind the mangers, where the horns of the cows pricked out of the obscurity. The child shrank, he balanced stiffly, rested the pan on the manger wall, and tipped out the food, half to this cow, half to the next....

1.　布朗溫哄孩子的方式很獨特，他帶着孩子去看他餵牛。孩子不再哭鬧了，他也在自己熟悉的勞作方式中得到了內心的寧靜。

2.　在靜謐的穀倉裏，小女孩看着爸爸餵乳牛，她進入了一個令她驚異的、全新的環境，於是漸漸忘記了剛才的不快，心情也煥然一新了。

3.　因為天氣很冷，布朗溫用一塊披肩裹着女兒。

六十七　哄孩子

　　布朗溫一手抱着孩子，開始給乳牛配料。他把切好的乾草、發過酵的穀粒和一點粗粉放在一個盆子裏，孩子十分驚奇地看着他幹活。在新的環境裏，她的體內萌發出了新的生命。狂風暴雨般的哭鬧過去了，但她的小身體時而還在餘波中抽搐、顫抖。她睜着大大的、好奇的眼睛，樣子很惹人愛憐。她一聲不吭，一動不動。

　　他彷彿身處夢境之中，一顆心沉到底部，表情則寧靜如水，他端着一盆飼料站了起來。他一手抱孩子，一手拿着盆，小心地保持着平衡。方形披肩的絲質流蘇輕輕地搖曳，穀粒和乾草掉了在地上。他順着牛槽後面昏暗的通道走過去，牛角從黑暗中豎起來，小女孩向後縮了縮，他僵直地站好身子，把盆放在食槽壁上，倒出飼料，一半給這頭乳牛，一半給另一頭。……

The journey had to be performed several times. There was the rhythmic sound of the shovel in the barn, then the man returned walking stiffly between the two weights, the face of the child peering out from the shawl. Then the next time, as he stooped, she freed her arm and put it round his neck, clinging soft and warm, making all easier.

D.H. Lawrence: <u>The Rainbow</u>

他這樣來回走了幾趟。先是聽到穀倉裏有鏟子發出有節奏的聲音，然後他雙手都拿着重物吃力地走回來，孩子的臉從披肩裏露出來。他再次彎下腰的時候，小女孩伸出一隻手，勾住了他的脖子，把柔軟而溫暖的身子靠在他胸前，這樣他幹起活來就更自如了。

(英) 勞倫斯：《彩虹》

68　I Must Be Off [1]

　　It was a hurried breakfast with no taste in it. I got up from the meal, saying with a sort of briskness, as if it had only just occurred to me, "Well! I suppose I must be off!" and then I kissed my sister, who was laughing, and nodding and shaking in her usual chair[2], and kissed Biddy[3], and threw my arms around Joe's neck. Then I took up my little portmanteau and walked out. The last I saw of them[4] was, when I presently heard a scuffle behind me, and looking back, saw Joe throwing an old shoe[5] after me and Biddy throwing another old shoe. I stopped then, to wave my hat, and dear old Joe waved his strong right arm above his head, crying huskily, "Hooroar[6]"! and Biddy put her apron to her face.

Charles Dickens: <u>Great Expectations</u>

---

1. 比普要去倫敦受 "上等人" 的教育了。本段是他與姐姐、姐夫 (Joe) 告別時的情景。
2. "姐姐" 已經精神失常。
3. 比蒂負責照顧 "姐姐"，後來嫁給了Joe。

六十八　告別

我匆匆吃完了早飯，真是食而不知其味。我站起身，擺出一副挺輕鬆的樣子，好像剛剛想起了一件事，"對了，我想我該走了！"然後，我吻了我姐姐，她坐在平常坐的那把椅子上，哈哈地笑着，不停地點着頭，身體搖來擺去。我又吻了比蒂，最後張開雙臂摟住了喬的脖子。隨後，我提起小手提箱，走了出去。沒走幾步，就聽到身後有腳步聲，回頭一望，只見喬朝我扔來一隻舊鞋，比蒂又扔出了另一隻。我站住了，向他們揮帽告別，我的老朋友喬將他那結實的右臂舉過頭頂揮動着，聲音嘶啞地喊道："好！"比蒂用圍裙捂住了臉。這就是我最後一眼看到的情景。

（英）狄更斯：《遠大前程》

----

4. The last I saw them：指最後看見他們的舉動。

5. throwing an old shoe：這是舊時英國鄉間的迷信習俗，扔舊鞋旨在祝遠行的人幸運。

6. Hooroar：＝ Hurrah，表示鼓勵的喝采聲。

69 Good-bye[1]

He went to the bed, removed one of the pair of pillows thereon, and flung it to the floor.

Sue looked at him, and bending over the bed-rail wept silently. "You don't see that it is a matter of conscience with me, and not of dislike to you!" she brokenly murmured. "Dislike to you ! But I can't say any more — it breaks my heart — it will be undoing all I have begun! Jude — good-night!"

"Good-night," he said, and turned to go.

"O but you shall kiss me!" said she, starting up. "I can't — bear — !"

He clasped her, and kissed her weeping face as he had scarcely ever done before, and they remained in silence till she said, "Good-bye, good-bye!" And then gently pressing him away she got free, trying to mitigate the sadness by saying: "We'll be dear friends just the same, Jude, won't we?

---

1. 淑和裘德在各自離婚後同居。他們的三個孩子自殺後,淑極度悔恨自卑,覺得他們的同居生活是褻瀆神聖的,於是決定離開裘德,回到前夫身邊。裘德感到十分痛心。本篇描述了他們分手時的傷感情景。

六十九　忍痛分手

　　他走到牀邊，抓起牀上一對枕頭中的一個，扔到了地板上。

　　淑看着他，俯在牀欄杆上，默默地流着淚。"你不明白，我這樣做是出於良心發現，而不是因為不喜歡你！"她輕聲地、斷斷續續地説。"不是不喜歡你！不過我不能再説下去了 —— 我的心都要碎了 —— 再説下去我就會回心轉意了！裴德 —— 再見吧！"

　　"再見，"裴德説完，轉身要走。

　　"哦，你得吻吻我！"她突然站起身來説，"我受不了 —— ！"

　　他把她摟在懷裏，吻着她那掛滿淚水的臉，他似乎從未這樣吻過她。兩人沉默了一會兒，最後她説，"再見！再見！"她輕輕地推開他，掙脱了他的懷抱。為了緩和這悲傷的氣氛，她又説："我們還會是親密的朋友，裴德，

And we'll see each other sometimes — Yes! — and forget all this, and try to be as we were long ago?"

Jude did not permit himself to speak, but turned and descended the stairs.

Thomas Hardy: Jude the Obscure

是不是？我們時不時還可以見見面 —— 我們會的！—— 忘
掉這一切，讓我們像很久以前那樣做表兄妹，好嗎？"

裘德忍着沒有再說甚麼，一轉身下了樓。

（英）哈代：《無名的裘德》

70 Into Each Hole a Woman Dropped a Seed

With their bare feet moving in step, the line of women walked and sang three times[1] around every farmer's field. Then they separated, and each woman fell in behind a farmer as he moved along each row, punching a hole in the earth every few inches with his big toe. Into each hole a woman dropped a seed, covered it over with her own big toe, and then moved on.

Alex Haley: Roots

---

1. sang three times：農婦們唱歌是在祈禱她們播下的種子能夠成活和生長。

七十　播種

　　排成一隊的婦女們光着腳齊步行進，在每個農民的田頭唱三遍歌，然後分散開，每個農婦走到一個農夫背後，跟着他沿着一行行的田壟向前移動。他每隔幾英寸就用大腳趾在土地上戳一個洞，農婦便往每一個洞裏撒下一粒種子，再用大腳趾撥土蓋上它，然後接着向前走。

　　　　　　　　　　　　（美）阿里克斯·哈利：《根》

71 Binding the Corn

Her binding proceeds with clock-like monotony. From the sheaf last finished she draws a handful of ears, patting their tips with her left palm to bring them even. Then stooping low she moves forward, gathering the corn with both hands against her knees, and pushing her left gloved hand under the bundle to meet the right on the other side, holding the corn in an embrace like that of a lover. She brings the ends of the bond[1] together, and kneels on the sheaf while she ties it, beating back her skirts now and then when lifted by the breeze. A bit of her naked arm is visible between the buff leather of the gauntlet and the sleeve of her gown; and as the day wears on[2] its feminine smoothness[3] becomes scarified by the stubble, and bleeds.

Thomas Hardy: <u>Tess of the d'Urbervilles</u>

---

1. bond：用那把麥子做的結紮物。
2. wears on：（時間）消逝。
3. its feminine smoothness：（指手臂）女性特有的光滑的皮膚。

七十一 捆麥

　　她捆麥的動作像鐘擺似的單調。她從剛打好的麥捆中抽出一把麥穗，用左手手掌把穗頭拍齊。然後彎下腰向前移動，用雙手將麥子攏向膝蓋，把帶着手套的左手插到麥捆下面，和另一面的右手合攏，像擁抱情人似的抱住麥捆；她把麥繩的兩頭拉到一起，跪在麥子上打捆。有時微風吹起她的裙子，她便用手撥回去。暗黃色的手套和衣袖之間，露出她的一小段手臂，時間久了，她嬌嫩的皮膚便被麥茬劃破，流出血來。

　　　　　　　　　　　　　(英) 哈代：《德伯家的苔絲》

72   A Spell

After a while, feeling very tired, it occurred to him that he deserved a spell and a smoke for five minutes. He closed the door and placed a pair of steps against it. There were two windows in the room almost opposite each other; these he opened wide in order that the smoke and smell of his pipe might be carried away. Having taken these precautions against surprise[1], he ascended to the top of the step ladder that he had laid against the door and sat down at ease. Within easy reach was the top of a cupboard where he had concealed a pint of beer in a bottle. To this he now applied himself. Having taken a long pull at the bottle, he tenderly replaced it on the top of the cupboard and proceeded to "hinjoy"[2] a quiet smoke, remarking to himself:

"This is where we get some of our own back[3]."

He held, however, his trowel[4] in one hand, ready for immediate action in case of interruption.

Robert Tressell: The Ragged Trousered Philanthropist

---

1. surprise：突然檢查。工頭不允許工人們幹活時休息，因此常常突然來檢查。

七十二　小憩

過了一會兒，他感到很累，覺得應該休息五分鐘，抽抽煙。他關上門，把一副梯子頂在上面。房間裏有兩扇幾乎對開的窗戶；他敞開窗戶，好讓煙霧和煙斗發出的氣味散出去。做好這些防範突然檢查的準備之後，他就爬到頂着門的梯子頂部舒適地坐了下來。他一伸手就可以夠着壁櫥的頂端，那裏他藏着一瓶一品脱的啤酒。他開始享用他的啤酒。他喝了一大口，輕輕地把瓶子放回壁櫥頂上，接着悠閒地抽起煙來，邊抽邊自言自語地説：

"這樣我們才能撈回一些來。"

但是他仍然一隻手拿着砌刀，萬一工頭闖進來，他就可以馬上開始工作。

（英）羅伯特·特雷塞爾：《穿破褲子的慈善家》

---

2. "hinjoy"：= enjoy

3. This is where we get some of our own back：指這樣才不至於被僱主剝削得太慘。

4. trowel：抹子，砌刀。這是一位建築工人，正在粉刷房間。

73 Before the First Stroke Had Died Away[1]

All hands[2] worked on in silence for some minute, until the church clock began to strike six. Before the first stroke had died away, Sandy Jim had loosed his plane and was reaching for his jacket; Wiry Ben had left a screw half driven in, and thrown his screw-driver into his tool-basket; Mum[3] Taft, who, true to his name, had kept silence throughout the previous conversation, had flung down his hammer as he was in the act of lifting it; and Seth, too, had straightened his back, and was putting out his hand towards his paper cap. Adam alone had gone on with his work as if nothing had happened.

George Eliot: <u>Adam Bede</u>

---

1. 收工的鐘聲剛一敲響，幾位木匠就扔掉了手中的工具。本篇生動形象地描繪了他們急於收工的心情。
2. hands：指工匠，是個借代修辭手法。

七十三 收工

　　所有的工匠都默不作聲了，接着幹活一會兒，直到教堂的鐘開始敲六點。第一下鐘聲的餘音未絕，桑迪·吉姆就放下了刨子，伸手去拿外套；沃利·倍恩剛把一個螺絲擰進去一半，就把螺絲刀扔進了工具籃裏；默默·塔夫特真是名副其實，別人談話時他一言不發，鐘響時，他正把錘子舉起，馬上就把它扔掉了；賽斯也直起了腰，正伸手去取他的工帽。只有亞當繼續工作，好像甚麼也沒有發生似的。

　　　　　　　　　　（英）喬治·艾略特：《亞當·比德》

3.　Mum：意為"無言的、沉默的"，他一言不發，所以說"默默·塔夫特"的名字是名副其實。前面的兩個木匠的名字也是類似的，都體現了他們的身體或性格特徵。Sandy 意為"淺棕色的"，這是此人頭髮的顏色。Wiry 是"精瘦"的意思，這是個體態輕盈的小個子。

74   The Boar-hunt[1]

Louis[2] showed all the bravery and expertness of an experienced huntsman; for, unheeding the danger, he rode up to the tremendous animal, which was defending itself with fury against the dogs, and struck him with his boar-spear; yet, as the horse shyed from the boar, the blow was not so effectual as either to kill or disable him. No effort could prevail on the horse to charge a second time; so that the King, dismounting, advanced on foot against the furious animal, holding naked in his hand one of those short, sharp, straight, and pointed swords, which huntsmen used for such encounters. The boar instantly quitted the dogs to rush on his human enemy, while the King, taking his station, and posting himself firmly, presented the sword, with the purpose of aiming it at the boar's throat, or rather chest, within the collar-bone; in which case the weight of the beast and the impetuosity of its career[3], would have served to accelerate

---

1. 本選段描繪法國國王路易十一在一次狩獵中與野豬搏鬥的情景。作者抓住狩獵者與獵物在生死搏鬥與對峙中的一舉一動進行描寫,形象生動地把獵殺野獸的場面呈現在讀者眼前。

七十四　獵捕野豬

　　路易是個富有經驗的獵手，既勇猛又老練。野豬正在拚命地抵擋着獵狗的進攻，他不顧危險，策馬衝向那隻兇猛的野獸，用長矛向牠刺去。但是他的馬受到了驚嚇，往旁邊一閃，這一刺並不十分有力，未能將野豬刺死或刺倒。無論路易怎樣努力，也不能令他的馬再次向野豬進攻，國王只好下了馬，手裏握着獵人在肉搏中使用的筆直、鋒利的短劍，徒步逼近那狂怒的野獸。野豬馬上撇下那羣獵狗，撲向進攻他的人。路易擺好姿勢，站穩當，握着短劍，對準野豬鎖骨附近的部位，準備刺牠的喉嚨或胸部。在這種情況下，野獸本身的重量和衝力，會增大短劍

---

2. Louis： 即法國國王路易十一。後文的 the King　和 the Monarch亦指同一人。

3. the impetuosity of its career：career 義 "狂奔、亂撞"；impetuosity義 "魯莽、急躁"。

its own destruction. But, owing to the wetness of the ground, the King's foot slipped, just as this delicate and perilous manoeuvre ought to have been accomplished, so that the point of the sword encountering the cuirass of bristles on the outside of the creature's shoulder, glanced off without making any impression, and Louis fell flat on the ground. This was so far fortunate for the Monarch, because the animal, owing to the King's fall, missed his blow in his turn, and in passing only rent with his tusk the King's short hunting-cloak, instead of ripping up his thigh. But when, after running a little ahead in the fury of his course, the boar turned to repeat his attack on the King at the moment when he was rising, the life of Louis was in imminent danger. At this critical moment, Quentin Durward[4], who had been thrown out in the chase by the slowness of his horse, but who, nevertheless, had luckily distinguished and followed the blast of the King's horn, rode up, and transfixed the animal with his spear.

Sir Walter Scott: <u>Quentin Durward</u>

---

4. Quentin Durward：王室衛隊的槍手。

的殺傷力。這種刺殺難度高，很危險，眼看成功在望的時候，國王的腳在潮濕的地上滑了一下，劍尖碰到了野豬肩部的硬毛，一擦而過，未造成任何損傷，而路易卻摔倒在地上。這樣一來倒也救了他，因為野豬也因此而撲了空，從國王身上一躍而過，牠的獠牙只是撕破了他的短獵裝，而未能撕裂他的大腿。野豬瘋狂地衝前幾步，又掉過頭來再次進攻，這個時候，國王正要站起來，他的生命岌岌可危。就在這緊急關頭，昆丁·德沃德趕到了，剛才因為馬跑得慢，他落了在後面，後來幸而聽到國王的號角聲，跟了上來。他衝上前來，用長矛刺穿了野豬的身體。

（英）司各特：《昆丁·德沃德》

75　Building a Fire[1]

　　... he turned aside to the bank, which he climbed. On top, tangled in the underbrush about the trunks of several small spruce trees, was a high-water deposit of dry fire-wood — sticks and twigs, principally, but also larger portions of seasoned branches and fine, dry, last-year's grasses. He threw down several large pieces on top of the snow. This served for a foundation and prevented the young flame from drowning itself in the snow it otherwise would melt. The flame he got by touching a match to a small shred of birch bark that he took from his pocket. This burned even more readily than paper. Placing it on the foundation, he fed the young flame with wisps of dry grass and with the tiniest dry twigs.

　　He worked slowly and carefully, keenly aware of his danger[2]. Gradually, as the flame grew stronger, he increased the size of the twigs with which he fed it.

Jack London: "To Build a Fire"

1.　本選段描繪一個人在荒野的雪地裏拾柴生火的情景。

七十五　生火

　　他轉向河岸，爬上去。岸上，在幾棵小雲杉的樹幹下的灌木叢中，纏繞着水漲時遺留下的乾木柴，大多是樹枝和小枝條，也有不少枯木和去年的、細細的乾草。他把幾條大一些的枯木扔在雪地上，用來做底座，這樣剛生起來的火就不會因積雪融化而熄滅。他從口袋裏掏出一小塊樺木皮，用火柴點燃。這比紙更容易燃燒。他把點燃的樹皮放在底架上，再往剛燃起的火苗裏添上一束束的乾草和極細小的枯枝。

　　他深知自己處境危險，慢慢地、小心翼翼地生着火。火苗越來越大了，他向裏面添加了一些大的枝條。……

傑克·倫敦：《生火》

---

2. his danger：“他”的腳已被雪水浸濕，在酷寒的雪地中，如果他不能迅速地生起一堆火，就會被凍死。

76   Writing[1]

Writing was a trying business to Charley[2], who seemed to have no natural power over a pen, but in whose hand every pen appeared to become perversely animated[3], and to go wrong and crooked, and to stop, and splash, and sidle into corners, like a saddle-donkey. It was very odd, to see what old letters Charley's young hand had made; they, so wrinkled, and shrivelled, and tottering; it, so plump and round. Yet Charley was uncommonly expert at other things, and has as nimble little fingers as I ever watched.

"Well, Charlie," said I, looking over a copy of the letter O in which it was presented as square, triangular, pear-shaped, and collapsed in all kinds of ways, "we are improving. If we only get to make it round, we shall be perfect, Charley."

Then I made one, and Charley made one, and the pen wouldn't join Charley's neatly, but twisted it up into a knot.

"Never mind, Charley, we shall do it in time."

---

1. 此段描寫一位少女練習寫字的情景。作者通過細緻的觀察，形象的語言，幽默的筆調，把她初學寫字的情景和神態刻劃得入木三分。
2. Charley：查蕾是"我"（埃絲特）的使女。
3. perversely animated：有悖常情地活動起來。

七十六　練字

　　寫字對查蕾來說是件頭痛的事；她似乎天生不會用
筆，每一支筆在她的手裏都像是中了邪似的，不聽使喚，
彎彎扭扭的，一會兒停住不動，一會兒墨水四濺，一會兒
又像上了鞍的驢子，直往角落裏鑽。真是很怪，查蕾稚嫩
的手寫出來的字卻個個老氣橫秋：滿臉皺紋，骨瘦如柴，
搖搖欲墜；而她的小手是胖胖的、圓圓的。然而查蕾做其
它事情的時候卻是得心應手，像她那樣靈巧的手指，我還
從來沒有見過。

　　我看了看查蕾抄寫的"0"字，有的寫成正方形，有的
寫成三角形，有的像個梨子，還有的東歪西倒。"好，查
蕾，"我說，"有進步，只要再寫得圓一點，就無可挑剔
了。"

　　接着我寫了一個"0"，查蕾也寫了一個，但她寫的那
個筆劃卻合不攏，歪歪扭扭的，像打了個結。

　　"沒關係，查蕾。很快就會寫好的。"

Charley laid down her pen, the copy being finished; opened and shut her cramped little hand; looked gravely at the page, half in pride and half in doubt; ...

Charles Dickens: <u>Bleak House</u>

查蕾練完字，放下筆，把她抽筋的小手，一張一合，
她嚴肅地望着自己寫的字，露出一副既自豪又懷疑的表
情……

　　　　　　　　（英）狄更斯：《荒涼山莊》

77　I Trip over a Word[1]

I come into the second-best parlor after breakfast, with my books, and an exercise-book, and a slate. My mother is ready for me at her writing-desk, but not half so ready as Mr. Murdstone[2] in his easy-chair by the window (though he pretends to be reading a book), or as Miss Murdstone, sitting near my mother stringing steel beads. The very sight of these two has such an influence over me, that I begin to feel the words I have been at infinite pains to get into my head, all sliding away, and going I don't know where. I wonder where they do go, by-the-by?

I hand the first book to my mother. Perhaps it is a grammar, perhaps a history, or geography. I take a last drowning look at the page as I give it into her hand, and start off aloud at a racing pace while I have got it fresh[3]. I trip over a word. Mr. Murdstone looks up. I trip over another

---

1. 大衛的繼父摩德斯通先生及其姐姐常常教訓大衛母子。在家中學習對大衛來說也變成一種折磨。
2. Murdstone：是 murder 和 stone 的諧音；暗示此人的性格陰險冷酷。
3. got it fresh：記憶猶新。

七十七　背書

　　早餐後我來到次好的客廳，拿着幾本書、一個練習簿和一塊寫字板。媽媽已經在寫字枱旁等我了，但是更急着等我的是坐在窗邊安樂椅上的摩德斯通先生（他假裝在看書），還有坐在媽媽旁邊串鋼珠子的摩德斯通小姐。一看到這兩個人，我便感到我辛辛苦苦裝進腦袋裏的那些詞都在悄悄地溜走，跑到我不知道的地方去了。順便提一句，我真的不清楚它們到底溜到哪裏去了。

　　我把第一本書遞給媽媽，那可能是本語法書，也可能是歷史書或地理書。我遞給她的時候，拚命地向那書頁瞥上最後一眼。然後趁自己還記得的時候，以飛快的速度高聲背誦起來。我背錯了一個詞，摩德斯通先生抬起頭來。

word. Miss Murdstone looks up. I redden, tumble over half-a-dozen words, and stop. I think my mother would show me the book if she dared, but she does not dare,...

Charles Dickens: *David Copperfield*

我又背錯了一個詞，摩德斯通小姐抬起頭來。我臉紅了，
又背錯了六、七個詞，停了下來。我想媽媽如果敢的話，
她會把那本書給我看的，可是她不敢，……

（英）狄更斯《大衛·科波菲爾》

78 Reading Passionately

One day a good fortune befell him, for he hit upon Lane's[1] translation of *The Thousand Nights and a Night*. He was captured first by the illustrations, and then he began to read, to start with, the stories that dealt with magic, and then the others; and those he liked he read again and again. He could think of nothing else. He forgot the life about him. He had to be called two or three times before he would come to his dinner. Insensibly he formed the most delightful habit in the world, the habit of reading: he did not know that thus he was providing himself with a refuge from all the distress of life; he did not know either that he was creating for himself an unreal world which would make the real world of every day a source of bitter disappointment. Presently he began to read other things. His brain was precocious....

---

1. Lane：Edward William Lane，英國的東方學者。

七十八　讀書

　　一天，菲利普十分走運，他偶然間找到了萊恩譯的
《一千零一夜》。開始時，插圖把他吸引住了，隨後他就讀
起了裏面的故事，先讀有關巫術的故事，然後就一篇一篇
的讀下去。對喜愛的章節，他看了一遍又一遍。其他的一
切他都置之度外，他忘卻了周圍的生活。吃飯的時候得讓
人招呼兩、三遍才姍姍而來。不知不覺地，他養成了世上
最令人愉悅的習慣——讀書：他並不知道這樣他就給自己
找到了躲避人生一切苦難的避難所，也沒有意識到他在給
自己築造一個虛幻的世界，從而使生活中真實的世界變成
痛苦失望的源泉。很快他開始閱讀其他書籍，他的智力過
早地成熟了。……

The summer was come now, and the gardener, an old sailor, made him a hammock and fixed it up for him in the branches of a weeping willow. And here for long hours he lay, hidden from anyone who might come to the vicarage[2], reading, reading passionately.

W. Somerset Maugham: Of Human Bondage

夏天來了，老水手出身的園丁給菲利普作了一個吊牀，掛在垂柳的樹枝上。他長時間地躺在那裏，躲開了牧師家的所有客人，如飢似渴地讀呀看呀。

（英）毛姆：《人性的枷鎖》

79　A Case to Examine[1]

Dr Tyrell[2] gave each of his clerks a case to examine.
The clerk took the patient into one of the inner rooms; they
were smaller, and each had a couch in it covered with black
horse-hair: he asked his patient a variety of questions,
examined his lungs, his heart, and his liver, made notes of
fact on the hospital letter, formed in his own mind some idea
of the diagnosis, and then waited for Dr Tyrell to come in.
This he did, followed by a small crowd of students, when he
had finished the men, and the clerk read out what he had
learned. The physician asked him one or two questions, and
examined the patient himself. If there was anything interesting
to hear students applied their stethoscope: you would see a
man with two or three to the chest, and two perhaps to his
back, while others waited impatiently to listen. The patient
stood among them a little embarrassed, but not altogether
displeased to find himself the centre of attention: he listened
confusedly while Dr Tyrell discoursed glibly on the case.

---

1. 此段描寫了醫科學生在門診實習時的情景。寥寥幾筆,就將醫生,實
   習學生與病人的神態躍然紙上。
2. Dr Tyrell:門診部的助理醫師,負責指導醫科實習生。

七十九　門診實習

　　蒂勒大夫讓他的每一個助手檢查一個病人。助手把病人帶到裏面的較小的房間裏，每個房間裏都放着一張躺椅，上面鋪着馬毛呢。助手向病人提出一連串的問題，隨後檢查他的肺部、心臟和肝臟，再將病情記在病歷卡上，並思考着如何診斷，然後他就等着蒂勒大夫進來。蒂勒大夫看完外面的男病人，就走了進來，身後跟着一小羣實習的學生。助手大聲唸出他的檢查結果，蒂勒大夫問他一、兩個問題，然後親自給病人做檢查。如果有甚麼值得一聽的東西，學生們便紛紛掏出聽診器，這時你便會看到有兩、三個學生在聽病人的胸部，可能還有另外兩個在聽他的背部，其他的學生則在旁急切地等待着輪到自己聽診。病人站在他們中間略顯尷尬，但作為這麼多人注意的焦點，也不會不高興。蒂勒大夫侃侃地描述着病情，病人聽

Two or three students listened again to recognize the murmur or the crepitation which the physician described, and then the man was told to put on his clothes.

W. Somerset Maugham: Of Human Bondage

得一頭霧水。兩、三個學生再次拿起聽診器，想辨別出大夫所講的雜音或沙沙聲。他們聽完後，才叫病人穿上衣服。

(英) 毛姆：《人性的枷鎖》

80 A Christmas Party (1)

When they had filled themselves up with the "cocoa-tea" and cakes and bread and jam, Elsie Linden and Nellie Newman helped to clear away the cups and saucers, and then Owen lit the candles on the Christmas tree and distributed the toys to the children, and a little while afterward Philpot — who had got a funny-looking mask out of one of the bonbons[1] — started a fine game pretending to be a dreadful wild animal which he called a Pandroculus[2], and crawling about on all fours[3], rolled his goggle eyes[4] and growled out he must have a little boy or girl to eat for his supper.

He looked so terrible that although they knew it was only a joke they were almost afraid of him, and ran away laughing and screaming to shelter themselves behind Nora or Owen; but all the same, whenever Philpot left off playing, they entreated him to "be it again", and so he had to keep on being a Pandroculus, until exhaustion compelled him to return to his natural form.

---

1. bonbons：亦做 cracker bonbon，彩包爆竹，聯歡會或宴會上裝有糖果、小飾物、箴言等的小禮包，抽開時作噼啪聲。

八十　聖誕晚會（一）

　　他們盡情地享用了"可可茶"、蛋糕、麵包、果醬之後，埃爾西·林登和尼利·紐曼幫忙把杯碟收走，然後歐文點燃聖誕樹上的蠟燭，把玩具分給孩子們。過了一會兒，菲爾波特 —— 他從彩包裏取出一個滑稽的面具 —— 裝扮成一個他稱之為潘卓庫勒斯的可怕的野獸，與孩子們做遊戲。他在地上爬來爬去，鼓鼓的眼珠骨碌碌地亂轉，咆哮着說他要抓一個小男孩或小女孩當晚飯吃。

　　他的樣子很嚇人，儘管孩子們知道只不過是在鬧着玩，還是有些害怕，他們笑着叫着跑開，躲在諾拉或歐文背後；可是每當菲爾波特一停下來，他們就會懇求他"再來一次！"他只好繼續扮成潘卓庫勒斯，直到精疲力盡，才摘掉面具，恢復了原形。

---

2. Pandroculus：這個編造出來的混合詞含有 Pan（希臘神話中的人身羊足的畜牧神）及 Dracula（吸血鬼）的意義，巧妙地表現出一隻猙獰怪獸的形象。

3. on all fours：用四肢爬行。

4. goggle eyes：突出的眼睛。

After this they all sat round the table and had a game of
cards; "Snap"[5], they called it, but nobody paid much attention
to the rules of the game: everyone seemed to think that the
principal thing to do was to kick up as much row as possible.
After a while Philpot suggested a change to "Beggar my
neighbour"[6], and won quite a lot of cards before they found
out that he had hidden all the jacks in the pocket of his coat,
and then they mobbed him for a cheat. He might have been
seriously injured if it had not been for Bert, who created a
diversion by standing on a chair and announcing that he was
about to introduce to their notice "Bert White's World-famed
Pandorama" as exhibited before all the nobility and crowned
heads of Europe, England, Ireland and Scotland, including
North America and Wales.

Robert Tressell: The Ragged Trousered Philanthropists

---

5. Snap：一種兒童玩的簡單牌戲，玩者各自將手中的牌一張張發放桌
   面，搶先認出兩張相同者即呼 "同" (snap)，桌面所有的牌便統歸先
   呼者。
6. Beggar my neighbour：一種以全部吃光對手的牌為勝的兒童牌戲。

這個遊戲之後，他們都圍坐在桌子旁打牌，他們稱之為呼"同"牌戲，但沒有人太在意遊戲規則，大家似乎都覺得盡情喧鬧一番才是主要的。過了一會兒，菲爾波特建議換個樣兒，玩"吃光"，他贏了很多牌之後，大家才發現他把所有的"J"都藏到他的大衣口袋裏了。孩子們便把他圍在當中，說他騙人。如果不是伯特出了個新花樣，他就會被狠揍一通了。伯特站在椅子上宣布：舉世聞名的"伯特·懷特活動畫片"即將開演，此套畫片曾在歐洲、英格蘭、愛爾蘭和蘇格蘭，以及北美、威爾士等地向所有的貴族和皇族演出過。

（英）羅伯特·特雷塞爾：《穿破褲子的慈善家》

81 A Christmas Party (2)

A round of applause for Bert concluded the Pandorama performance; the lamp and the candles of the Christmas tree were re-lit — for although all the toys had been taken off, the tree still made a fine show with the shining glass ornaments — and then they had some more games; blind man's buff[1], a tug-of-war[2], — in which Philpot was defeated with great slaughter[3] — and a lot of other games. And when they were tired of these, each child "said a piece" or sung a song, learnt specially for the occasion.

...

Most of them were by this time quite tired out, so after some supper the party broke up. Although they were nearly all very sleepy, none of them were very willing to go,...

...

---

1. blind man's buff：捉迷藏（一人蒙着眼去捉在他周圍來回躲閃的人，捉後辨認所捉之人是誰）。

2. a tug-of-war：拔河

3. defeated with great slaughter：（俗語）完全輸了。slaughter：慘敗。

八十一　聖誕晚會（二）

伯特的活動畫片表演結束時，響起了一片掌聲。燈和聖誕樹上的蠟燭又亮了，儘管所有的玩具都拿了下來，聖誕樹上還掛着許多光閃閃的玻璃飾物，仍然十分好看。接着他們又玩了捉迷藏、拔河和其他很多遊戲，拔河時菲爾波特一敗塗地。這些玩夠了之後，每個孩子背誦一首詩或者唱一首歌，這都是他們特意為這個晚會準備的。

……

這時大家差不多都累壞了，所以吃了些夜宵之後，晚會就結束了。雖然幾乎每個人都很睏倦，但大家都不大願意離開，……

……

As they were going down the stairs Frankie held a hurried consultation with his mother, with the result that he was able to shout after them an invitation to come again next Christmas.

Robert Tressell: The Ragged Trousered Philanthropists

他們下樓的時候，小弗蘭克匆匆跟母親商量了一下，
然後就在他們身後大聲喊叫，邀請他們明年聖誕節再來。

(英) 羅伯特·特雷塞爾：《穿破褲子的慈善家》

82 Afternoon Tea

From five o'clock to eight is on certain occasions a little eternity; but on such an occasion[2] as this the interval could be only an eternity of pleasure. The persons concerned in it were taking their pleasure quietly, ...

The shadows on the perfect lawn were straight and angular; they were the shadows of an old man sitting in a deep wicker-chair near the low table on which the tea had been served, and of two younger men strolling to and fro, in desultory talk, in front of him. The old man had his cup in his hand; it was an unusually large cup, of a different pattern from the rest of the set and painted in brilliant colours. He disposed of its contents[3] with much circumspection, holding it for a long time close to his chin, with his face turned to the house. His companions had either finished their tea or were indifferent to their privilege; they smoked cigarettes as they continued to stroll.

Henry James: The Portrait of a Lady

---

1. 本篇描繪了英國特有的習俗——下午茶的一個場面。茶會在住宅前的草坪上舉行，參加者在一起喝喝茶，吃些點心，聊聊天，這是較為典型的英國下午茶。

八十二　下午茶

　　有的時候，從五點到八點這幾個小時似乎是漫長無盡的。但在這樣一種場合，這段時間只會給予人們無盡的快樂。參加此茶會的人正在靜靜地享用這種快樂……。

　　精美的草坪上有幾條影子，直直的，有稜有角。其中一條影子是一位老人的，他坐在一把扶手高高的柳條椅上，旁邊有一張矮矮的桌子，上面擺着茶點；另外兩條影子是兩位年輕男士的，他們在老人面前來回漫步，隨意交談。老人手裏拿着一隻特別大的茶杯，色彩鮮艷奪目，樣式與其它茶具不同。他喝茶的時候小心翼翼，久久地把茶杯端在嘴邊，眼睛注視着那幢房子。他的兩位同伴可能已經喝完了茶，或者對這種享受不大感興趣；他們一面繼續散步，一面抽着煙。

（美）亨利・詹姆斯：《一位女士的畫像》

---

2. such an occasion： 指這個茶會。
3. disposed of its contents： 喝盡茶杯裏的茶。

83 Playing Charades[1]

Ere long, a bell tinkled, and the curtain drew up. Within the arch, the bulky figure of Sir George Lynn, whom Mr Rochester had likewise chosen,[2] was seen enveloped in a white sheet: before him, on a table, lay open a large book; and at his side stood Amy Eshton, draped in Mr Rochester's cloak, and holding a book in her hand. Somebody unseen, rang the bell merrily; then Adèle (who had insisted on being one of her guardian's[3] party), bounded forward, scattering round her the contents of a basket of flowers she carried on her arm. Then appeared the magnificent figure of Miss Ingram, clad in white, a long veil on her head, and a wreath of roses round her brow; by her side walked Mr Rochester, and together they drew near the table. They knelt; while Mrs

---

1. 猜啞劇字謎。本篇寫的是羅切斯特先生家名流聚會的一個場面。大家分成兩組，一組進行短暫的表演，另一組根據其動作和場景猜出字謎。

232

八十三　猜字謎

　　不久，鈴聲響了，帷幕拉了起來。也被羅切斯特選中
的喬治·林恩伯爵的笨重身軀，出現在拱門裏，他身上裹着
一條白單子；他面前的桌子上，放着一本打開的大書。他
的旁邊站着愛米·埃什頓，她披着羅切斯特先生的斗蓬，手
中拿着一本書。從看不見的地方響起了歡快的鈴聲。然後
阿黛爾（她堅持要加入羅切斯特先生這一組）蹦蹦跳跳地
跑了出來，她手臂上挎着一個籃子，把裏面的花兒撒在周
圍。接着，英格拉姆小姐那優美的身形出現了，她一身潔
白，一塊面紗從頭上垂下，額上繞着一個玫瑰花環；羅切
斯特先生與她並肩走過來，他們一起走到桌邊，跪下。同

---

2. 羅切斯特先生挑選了幾個人與他同組，其中就有喬治·林恩伯爵。

3. her guardian：阿黛爾的監護人，即羅切斯特先生。

Dent and Louisa Eshton, dressed also in white, took up their stations behind them. A ceremony followed, in dumb show, in which it was easy to recognize the pantomime of a marriage. At its termination, Colonel Dent and his party consulted in whispers for two minutes, then the Colonel called out —

"Bride!" Mr Rochester bowed, and the curtain fell.

Charlotte Brontë: Jane Eyre

樣是一身白色裝束的丹特太太和露易莎·埃什頓站在他們後面。然後他們表演了一個無聲的儀式，很容易看出是婚禮的啞劇。表演結束後，丹特上校與他同組的人低聲商量了兩分鐘，接着喊道：

"新娘！"羅切斯特先生一鞠躬表示認可，帷幕落了下來。

（英）夏洛蒂·勃朗特：《簡·愛》

84 The *Acziavimas*[1]

The *acziavimas* is a ceremony which, once begun, will continue for three or four hours, and it involves one uninterrupted dance. The guests form a great ring, locking hands, and, when the music starts up, begin to move around in a circle. In the centre stands the bride, and, one by one, the men step into the enclosure and dance with her. Each dances for several minutes — as long as he pleases; it is a very merry proceeding[2], with laughter and singing, and when the guest has finished, he finds himself face to face with Teta Elzbieta[3], who holds the hat. Into it he drops a sum of money — a dollar, or perhaps five dollars, according to his power, and his estimate of the value of the privilege. The guests are expected to pay for this entertainment; if they be proper guests, they will see that there is a neat sum[4] left over for the bride and bridegroom to start life upon.

Upton Sinclair: <u>The Jungle</u>

---

1. *acziavimas*：這是立陶宛 (Luthuania) 式婚宴上的一個重要儀式。
   acziavimas 是立陶宛語。
2. proceeding：過程，舉動。

八十四　婚宴上的舞蹈

　　acziavimas 這種儀式一開始，便要持續三、四個小時，儀式本身是一種不間斷的舞蹈。賓客們手拉手圍成一個大圈子，音樂一奏響，就開始轉圈。新娘站在中間，男士們挨個走進圈內與她跳舞。每人跳幾分鐘 —— 長短隨意；這是個充滿歡樂的時光，笑聲、歌聲不斷。每個來賓跳完舞，便會發現伊莎比塔大娘拿着帽子站在他面前。他往裏面放一點錢 —— 或許一元，或許五元，這要看他的經濟能力以及他對享有這參與特權的估價。客人參加這項娛樂活動是要付錢的；如果是較得體的客人，便會想着多留點兒錢，好讓新郎和新娘開始過日子。

　　　　　　　　　　　　(美) 厄普頓·辛克萊：《屠場》

3.　Teta Elzbieta：新娘奧娜的繼母，這場婚禮由她主辦。
4.　a neat sum：一筆數目不小的錢。

85   A Real Bully Circus[1]

It was a real bully circus. It was the splendidest sight
that ever was, when they all came riding in, two and two, a
gentleman and lady, side by side, the men just in their drawers
and under-shirts, and no shoes nor stirrups, and resting their
hands on their thighs, easy and comfortable — there must a
been[2] twenty of them — and every lady with a lovely
complexion, and perfectly beautiful, and looking just like a
gang of real sure-enough queens, and dressed in clothes that
cost millions of dollars, and just littered with diamonds. It
was a powerful fine sight; I never see anything so lovely.
And then one by one they got up and stood, and went a-
weaving around the ring so gentle and wavy and graceful,
the men looking ever so tall and airy and straight, with their
heads bobbing and skimming along, away up there under
the tent-roof, and every lady's rose-leafy dress flapping soft
and silky around her hips, and she looking like the most
loveliest parasol.

---

1. 這是一篇描寫馬戲表演的文字。作者以天真爛漫的少年的目光和口
    吻，對馬戲演員的容貌體態，以及人和馬的每一個動作，都作了精彩
    的描寫，語言形象生動，趣味盎然。
2. must a been：（方言）＝ must have been

八十五　馬戲表演

　　這個馬戲班棒極了。當他們一男一女、一對對並排着騎馬入場的時候，那場景真是壯觀極了。男演員 —— 估計有二十人 —— 只穿着內衣內褲，沒有穿鞋，也沒拿馬刺，兩手放在大腿上，瀟灑自如；每個女演員都是貌若桃花，美如天仙，看上去像一羣地地道道、不折不扣的皇后，穿着價值連城、鑲滿鑽石的服裝。如此懾人的漂亮場景，我還是頭一次看見。然後他們一個接一個地從馬背上站了起來，一圈又一圈地繞着表演場轉，既輕且柔，如波似浪，十分優美。男演員們看上去高大、輕盈、挺拔，他們的頭部一上一下的飄過去，高得接近了帳篷的頂部。每位女演員的裙裾像玫瑰花瓣，柔軟而光滑，在臀上一起一落，她們看上去就像一頂頂美麗絕頂的陽傘。

And then faster and faster they went, all of them dancing, first one foot stuck out in the air and then the other, the horses leaning more and more, and the ring-master going round and round the centre-pole, cracking his whip and shouting "Hi!-hi!" and the clown cracking jokes behind him; and by-and-by all hands dropped the reins, and every lady put her knuckles on her lips and every gentleman folded his arms, and then how the horses did lean over and hump themselves! And so, one after the other they all skipped off into the ring, and made the sweetest bow I ever see, and then scampered out, and everybody clapped their hands and went just about wild.

Mark Twain: The Adventures of Huckleberry Finn

接着他們越跑越快，所有的人都跳起舞來，先把一隻腳伸到空中，然後又伸出另一隻，馬身傾斜得越來越厲害。馬戲團的領班繞着中心柱子走來走去，打着響鞭，嘴裏喊着："嗨！嗨！"，還有個小丑跟在他後面講着笑話。過了一會兒，每個人都扔掉了韁繩，女演員把雙手放在唇邊，男演員將雙臂抱在胸前，那些馬側身弓背，那樣子真令人叫絕。隨後，他們一個接一個地縱身跳到表演場裏，向大家鞠躬致意，那姿勢真是優美透頂。然後他們蹦蹦跳跳地退了場。人人都發狂似地鼓掌。

　　　　（美）馬克·吐溫：《哈克貝利·費恩歷險記》

86 Packed Solid with People[1]

...the square in front of the palace, packed solid with people, presented the appearance of a sea, with five or six streets flowing into it, constantly disgorging a stream of heads. The waves of this sea broke against the corners of the houses jutting out like promontories into the irregular basin of the square. Shouts, laughter and the shuffling of thousands of feet blended to produce a mighty uproar.

Victor Hugo: The Hunchback of Notre Dame

---

1. 本選段描繪了十五世紀的巴黎人慶祝一月六日顯現節 (Epiphany) 和愚人節的盛大場面。顯現節是耶穌基督第一次顯現給以東方三博士為代表的非猶太人的慶祝活動日。這一天也是愚人節，Festival of Fools。這天，司法宮要上演聖蹟劇，還要推選愚人王，因此熱鬧非凡。

八十六　人聲鼎沸

　　司法宮前的廣場擠滿了人，看上去像一片汪洋大海，五、六條街道就像支流，不斷地將人流吐入大海。周圍的建築物像海岬般伸進不平整的廣場中，那片人海不時地拍打着屋角。成千上萬人的喊聲、笑聲、腳步聲混雜交織，廣場上人聲鼎沸。

（法）雨果：《鐘樓駝俠》

87 Buffoonery[1]

...At one and the same moment there had risen above the shoulders of the crowd, nearly opposite Mr Brooke, and within ten yards of him, the effigy of himself; buff-coloured waistcoat, eye-glass, and neutral physiognomy, painted on rag; and there had arisen apparently in the air, like the note of the cuckoo, a parrot-like, Punch[2]-voiced echo of his words. Everybody looked up at the open windows in the houses at the opposite angles of the converging streets; but they were either blank, or filled by laughing listeners....

"Buffoonery, tricks, ridicule the test of truth — all that is very well" — here an unpleasant egg broke on Mr Brooke's shoulder, as the echo said, "All that is very well"; then came a hail of eggs, chiefly aimed at the image, but occasionally hitting the original[3], as if by chance. There was a stream of

---

1. 布魯克先生是市府議員的候選人。在他進行競選演說時，敵對的選民演出了一場惡作劇。本選段將這種典型的競選混亂場面描繪得栩栩如生。
2. Punch：潘奇，英國傳統的滑稽木偶劇 *Punch and Judy* 中的男主角，是個勾鼻、駝背的滑稽木偶。
3. the original：原形，指布魯克先生本人。

八十七　鬧劇

……同一時候，離布魯克先生不到十碼遠，幾乎在他正對面，在人羣的頭頂上出現了他的模擬像；模擬像畫在一塊破布上，穿上暗黃色的背心，戴着眼鏡，臉上沒有表情；與此同時，空中還響起了模仿他講話的聲音，相當清晰，像布穀鳥的叫聲，又像鸚鵡學舌，以滑稽木偶的腔調重複他的話。大家都抬起頭，向十字路口那些遙遙相對的敞開的窗戶張望，但是有的窗口沒有人，有的擠滿了哈哈大笑的聽眾。
　　……

　　"無理取鬧、惡作劇、冷嘲熱諷，都是對真理的考驗——這一切都很好"這時，一隻討厭的雞蛋啪的一聲打在布魯克先生的肩膀上，那個聲音又在模仿他的話，"這一切都很好"；接着一連串的雞蛋擲了過來，大部分打在模擬像上，但似乎是出於偶然也有幾個打中了布魯克先生本

new men pushing among the crowds; whistles, yells, bellowings, and fifes made all the greater hubbub because there was shouting and struggling to put them down. No voice would have had wing enough to rise above the uproar[4], and Mr Brooke, disagreeably anointed[5], stood his ground[6] no longer.

George Eliot: <u>Middlemarch</u>

---

4. No voice ... had wing enough to rise above the uproar：這裏用了比擬修辭，指沒有聲音高於那喧鬧聲，正如沒有雀鳥有足夠羽翼飛得更高一樣。

5. anointed：這個詞語帶相關，既可解作塗了油污，亦可解作塗了聖油。這裏含有諷刺意味。

6. stood his ground：堅持立場。

人。這時，又來了另一隊人，在人羣中擠來擠去，口哨聲、喊聲、吼叫聲、笛子聲響成一片，再加上一些人大聲喊叫着試圖控制這個局面，會場上更加混亂不堪了。誰的聲音也壓不住這種喧鬧聲，而布魯克先生身上污糟一片，只好退了下去。

(英) 喬治·艾略特：《米德爾馬契》

88 Preaching[1]

... the preacher was lining out a hymn. He lined out two lines, everybody sung it, and it was kind of grand to hear it, there was so many of them and they done it in such a rousing way; then he lined out two more for them to sing — and so on. The people woke up more and more, and sung louder and louder; and towards the end some begun to groan, and some begun to shout. Then the preacher begun to preach, and begun in earnest, too; and went weaving first to one side of the platform and then the other, and then a-leaning down over the front of it, and his arms and his body going all the time, and shouting his words out with all his might; and every

---

1. 本篇中作者通過少年的眼光，用詼諧的語言對牧師及信徒們的神情、舉止作了生動的刻劃。另外，作者用重複的詞彙，簡單的句式，句與句間重複運用 "and"、"then" 接成並列句，加上一些錯誤語法如 "began" 誤為 "begun"、"sang" 誤為 "sung"、"did" 誤為 "done" 等，都有意模仿小說的主人公，一個未受過良好教育的孩子的口吻，以求語言的真實感。

八十八　布道

　　牧師正在領唱聖歌。他先唱兩行，大家再跟着唱，聽
上去頗為雄壯；這裏有這麼多人，唱得又是這麼振奮人
心。然後他又領着大家唱了兩句，就這樣一直唱下去。人
們越來越振作，聲音越來越大；快到最後時，有人開始哼
哼，有人開始喊叫。接着牧師就開始布道，語調十分誠
懇；他搖着身子走到台子的這一邊，又走到另一邊，然後
在台前彎下身子，雙臂和身體都向前伸，用盡全力叫喊

now and then he would hold up his Bible and spread it open, and kind of pass it around this way and that, shouting, "It's the brazen serpent in the wilderness! Look upon it and live!²" And people would shout out, "Glory! — A-a-men!" And so he went on, and the people groaning and crying and saying amen...

Mark Twain: The Adventures of Huckleberry Finn

---

2. 此句出自《舊約·民數記》第二十一章。百姓埋怨神和摩西,把他們從埃及帶到曠野裏,沒有糧,沒有水。於是耶和華使火蛇進入他們中間,咬他們。百姓求摩西禱告耶和華叫這些蛇離開。於是摩西為百姓禱告。耶和華對摩西説:"你製造一條火蛇,掛在竿子上;凡被蛇咬的,一望這蛇,就必得活。"摩西就製造一條銅蛇,掛在竿子上;凡被蛇咬的,一望這銅蛇,就活了。

着。他不時地舉起聖經，將它攤開，好像要遞給這邊的人看，然後又遞到另一邊，他喊道："這是荒野中的銅蛇！看看它就可以活下去！"眾人就喊："榮耀啊！阿——阿們！"他就這樣説下去，那些人哼着叫着，喊着"阿們"……

(美) 馬克・吐溫：《哈克貝利・費恩歷險記》

89   He Flung Himself upon the Crucifix[1]

The frenzied laughter died on Arthur's lips. He snatched up the hammer from the table and flung himself upon the crucifix.

With the crash that followed he came suddenly to his senses, standing before the empty pedestal, the hammer still in his hand, and the fragments of the broken image scattered on the floor about his feet.

He threw down the hammer. "So easy!" he said and turned away. "And what an idiot I am!"

E.L. Voynich: <u>*The Gadfly*</u>

---

1. 牛虻認識到了神父的虛偽和卑鄙。砸神像標誌着他擺脫教會、開始新
生活的決心。

八十九　砸神像

　　瘋狂的笑從亞瑟的唇上消失了。他抓起桌子上的那把
鎚子，向耶穌十架受難像撲過去。

　　隨着"嘩啦"的響聲，他猛醒過來，手仍拿着鎚子，
站在空空的底座前，神像的碎片散落在他腳旁的地板上。

　　他扔掉了鎚子："這麼容易！"他說，轉過身去。
"我真是個傻瓜！"

（英）伏尼契：《牛虻》

90 He Stood Elevated in the Witness-box[1]

He stood elevated in the witness-box, with burning cheeks in a cool lofty room: the big framework of punkahs[2] moved gently to and fro high above his head, and from below many eyes were looking at him out of dark faces, out of white faces, out of red faces, out of faces attentive, spellbound, as if all these people sitting in orderly rows upon narrow benches had been enslaved by the fascination of his voice. It was very loud, it rang startling in his own ears, it was the only sound audible in the world, for the terribly distinct questions that extorted his answers seemed to shape themselves in anguish and pain within his breast — came to him poignant and silent like the terrible questioning of one's conscience. Outside the court the sun blazed — within was the wind of great punkahs that made you shiver, the shame that made you burn, the attentive eyes whose glance stabbed. The face

---

1. 吉姆是帕特納號船上的大副。有一次輪船途中觸礁，吉姆和船長等人丟下全船旅客逃命，但他一直受着良心的譴責，在法庭調查事實時，他鼓足勇氣説出了真相。本篇即描述了他在法庭作證講述沉船真相時的情景。

2. punkahs：流行在印度等地區，懸在天花板上的布屏風扇。

254

九十　法庭作證

　　吉姆高高地站在證人席裏。儘管這房子房頂很高，十分涼爽，他卻滿臉通紅。高懸在他頭頂上的大大的吊扇，緩緩地轉來轉去，下面有很多雙眼睛注視着他，那些面孔有黑的、白的、紅的，專注的、出神的，好像那些整齊地坐在窄凳上的人，都被他富有魅力的聲音迷住了。那聲音很響亮，他自己聽起來都有些驚訝，覺得那是世界上唯一可聽到的聲音。那些他不能不回答的明明白白的問題，令他心裏痛苦難堪 —— 有如對良心的厲害的譴責，既無聲又尖刻。法庭外面陽光熾熱 —— 法庭裏面，大型吊扇吹得你發抖，羞愧令你渾身發燒，聚精會神的目光像利劍刺

of the presiding magistrate, clean shaved and impassible, looked at him deadly pale between the red faces of the two nautical assessors. The light of a broad window under the ceiling fell from above on the heads and shoulders of the three men, and they were fiercely distinct in the half-light of the big court-room where the audience seemed composed of staring shadows. They wanted facts. Facts! They demanded facts from him, as if facts could explain anything!

Joseph Conrad: <u>*Lord Jim*</u>

痛了你。法庭庭長注視着吉姆，他那張刮得乾乾淨淨的臉上毫無表情；在兩個航事顧問的紅臉之間，他的臉顯得死一樣的蒼白。從天花板下那張大窗戶射入的光綫，照在這三個人的頭和肩上，在光綫不足的大法庭裏，他們的身形顯得格外清晰。相形之下，聽眾只算是一羣瞪着眼睛的影子罷了。他們要事實。事實！他們要他講出事實，好像事實能夠解釋一切。

(英) 康拉德：《吉姆爺》

91 The Verdict[1]

One o'clock struck as the jurors withdrew to their room. Not one woman had left her seat; several men had tears in their eyes. At first there was animated conversation, but then, as time went by and the jury did not return with the verdict, the general fatigue gradually began to calm the crowd of spectators. It was a solemn moment; the light in the courtroom had grown dimmer. Julien, extremely weary, heard people around him discussing whether this delay was a good or a bad sign. He saw with pleasure that everyone was on his side; the jury had not returned, and still not a single woman had left the room.

Just after two o'clock a great stir was heard. The little door of the jury room was opened and the Baron de Valenod stepped forward with a solemn, theatrical tread, followed by all the other jurors. He coughed, then declared that on his soul and conscience the unanimous verdict of the jury was that Julien Sorel was guilty of murder, and premeditated murder. This verdict entailed[2] the death sentence; it was pronounced a moment later.

Henri Beyle Stendhal: The Red and the Black

九十一 裁決

　　陪審員退庭出去商議的時候，時鐘正敲響一點。沒有一個婦女離開座位，幾位男士眼裏含着淚水。起初，大家談得很起勁；可是陪審團的裁決久候不至，眾人漸漸感到疲憊，慢慢安靜下來。這時的氣氛莊嚴肅穆，法庭裏的光綫也昏暗下來了。于連十分疲倦，他聽到周圍的人議論紛紛，猜測這拖延是好兆還是凶兆。他很高興看到所有的人都支持他。陪審團還沒有回來，也沒有一個婦女離開大廳。

　　兩點鐘剛過，法庭上一陣騷動。陪審團房間的小門打開了，德・瓦倫諾男爵邁着威嚴的台步走了出來，其餘陪審員全部跟在後面。他清清嗓子，然後宣布：根據天理良心，陪審團一致認為于連・索雷爾犯有殺人罪，而且是預謀殺人，這項罪名必然判處死刑。片刻之後就宣布了死刑。

（法）斯丹達爾：《紅與黑》

---

1. 于連預謀殺害瑞那夫人，受到了法庭的審判。本篇對陪審團作出裁決之前法庭裏焦急等待的氣氛以及法官宣布裁決的神態均作了細膩的描述。

2. entailed：使……成為必要。

259

92 Stood Fully Revealed before the Crowd[1]

She bore in her arms a child, a baby of some three months old, who winked and turned aside its little face from the too vivid light of day; because its existence, heretofore[2], had brought it acquainted only with[3] the gray twilight of a dungeon, or other darksome apartment of the prison.

When the young woman — the mother of this child — stood fully revealed before the crowd, it seemed to be her first impulse to clasp the infant closely to her bosom; not so much by an impulse of motherly affection, as that she might thereby conceal a certain token, which was wrought[4] or fastened into her dress. In a moment, however, wisely judging that one token of her shame would but poorly serve to hide another, she took the baby on her arm, and, with a burning

---

1. 海絲特‧普林因通姦罪而受監禁，這天要被帶到刑台上罰站示眾。這一段描述了她走出監獄大門時的情景。
2. heretofore：（正式用語）= hitherto，義為迄今為止。
3. acquainted... with：了解，熟悉。
4. wrought：（work 的過去分詞）製作的。

九十二　走出獄門

　　她懷裏抱着一個大約三個月大的嬰兒，這孩子眨着眼，把小臉扭到一旁，避開白天那過於耀眼的光綫；　因為自從來到人世，她一直生活在監牢或其他暗室的昏暗之中。

　　當這個年輕女子 —— 也就是這個孩子的母親 —— 完全站到人羣面前時，她的第一個衝動似乎是把嬰兒緊緊抱到胸前，這與其說是母愛的衝動，不如說是想藉此來掩蓋那繡在或釘在她衣服上的標記。然而她馬上意識到，這孩子也是一個恥辱的標記，用她來掩飾另一個恥辱是無濟於事的，因而她乾脆用一隻手臂抱着孩子，儘管滿臉通紅，

blush, and yet a haughty smile, and a glance that would not be abashed, looked around at her townspeople and neighbors. On the breast of her gown, in fine red cloth, surrounded with an elaborate embroidery and fantastic flourishes[5] of gold-thread, appeared the letter A[6].

Nathaniel Hawthorne: <u>The Scarlet Letter</u>

---

5. fantastic flourishes：奇妙的花飾。flourish：花體字的花飾。
6. the letter A：A 代表 adultery（通姦）。

卻面帶高傲的微笑，以毫無羞愧的目光環視着周圍的鎮民和她的街坊鄰居。她衣裙的胸前，露出了一個用紅色細布做成的字母 A，周圍用金色絲綫精心繡成了奇妙的花飾。

(美) 霍桑：《紅字》

93　He Turned toward the Scaffold[1]

He still walked onward, if that movement could be so described, which rather resembled the wavering effort of an infant, with its mother's arms in view, outstretched to tempt him forward. And now, almost imperceptible as were the latter steps[2] of his progress, he had come opposite the well-remembered and weather-darkened scaffold, where, long since, with all that dreary lapse of time between, Hester Prynne had encountered the world's ignominious stare. There stood Hester, holding little Pearl by the hand! And there was the scarlet letter on her breast! The minister here made a pause; although the music still played the stately and rejoicing march to which the procession moved[3]. It summoned him onward, — onward to the festival! — but here he made a pause.

... He turned toward the scaffold, and stretched forth his arms.

---

1. 珠兒的生父迪姆代爾牧師不敢公開懺悔自己的罪孽，但內心的譴責折磨了他整整七年。在他奄奄一息的時候，他終於下決心走上刑台，坦露自己胸膛上的紅字。

2. almost imperceptible as were the latter steps："後來的步伐差不多難以察覺"，指步伐很慢。

九十三　走向刑台

他還在向前"走"——如果我們能把他那種動作描述為"走"的話——但毋寧說他像一個嬰兒,看到媽媽伸出雙臂鼓勵他向前,便搖搖挄挄地往前走。他十分緩慢地繼續移動着腳步,來到了刑台的前面,這個令他難以忘卻的刑台,經過風吹日曬已經發黑。多年以前,海絲特・普林曾在那裏面對世人輕辱的白眼,從那以後,多少個腥風苦雨的日子已流逝而過。而現在,海絲特手拉着小珠兒站在旁邊,她的胸前帶着紅字。牧師停住了,而軍樂隊仍然演奏着威嚴而歡快的進行曲,遊行隊伍隨着樂曲繼續前進。音樂召喚他向前走,前去赴會,但他卻停住了。

……

……他面向刑台,伸出雙臂。

3.　the music... the procession moved：這天是慶祝選舉日,因此舉行了盛大的遊行。music：指軍樂。

"Hester," said he, "come hither[4]! Come, my little Pearl!"

...

He again extended his hand to the woman of the scarlet letter.

"... Come, Hester, come. Support me up yonder[5] scaffold!"

... They behold the minister, leaning on Hester's shoulder, and supported by her arm around him, approach the scaffold, and ascend its steps; while still the little hand of the sin-born child was clasped in his. Old Roger Chillingworth[6] followed, as one intimately connected with the drama of guilt and sorrow in which they had all been actors and well entitled[7], therefore, to be present at its closing scene.

Nathaniel Hawthorne: <u>The Scarlet Letter</u>

---

4. hither：（舊用法）向此處。

5. yonder：（舊用法）那邊的。

6. old Roger Chillingworth：他是海絲特的前夫，一直在暗中折磨牧師，使他多年來承受着內心的煎熬，以此復仇。

7. well entitled：有足夠資格的。

"海絲特，"他喊道，"過來呀！來呀，我的小珠兒！"

……

他又向帶着紅字的女人伸出手臂。

"……來，海絲特，過來呀。扶我上刑台！"

……眾人注視着牧師，他靠在海絲特的肩膀上，由她攙扶着走近刑台登上梯級，牧師的手中還牽着那個因罪孽而出生的孩子。而與這齣罪惡和痛苦的戲劇聯繫密切的老羅傑·奇林沃斯也跟在後面，他都是劇中的主要演員，在這最後一幕中便理所當然地登場了。

(美) 霍桑：《紅字》

94 An Execution

He stood and faced them, smiling, and the carbines shook in their hands.

"I am quite ready," he said.

...

"Ready — present — fire!"

The Gadfly staggered a little and recovered his balance. One unsteady shot had grazed his cheek, and a little blood fell on to the white cravat. Another ball had struck him above the knee. When the smoke cleared away the soldiers looked and saw him smiling still and wiping the blood from his cheek with the mutilated hand.

"A bad shot, men!" he said; and his voice cut in, clear and articulate, upon the dazed stupor of the wretched soldiers. "Have another try."

...

The smoke cleared slowly away, floating up into the glimmer of the early sunlight; and they saw that the Gadfly had fallen; and saw, too, that he was still not dead. For the first moment soldiers and officials stood as if they had been turned to stone, and watched the ghastly thing that writhed and struggled on the ground; then both doctor and colonel

九十四　槍決

　　牛虻站在那裏，面對着士兵，臉帶微笑。卡賓槍在士兵的手中顫動着。

　　"我已經完全準備好了。"他説。

　　……

　　"預備 —— 瞄準 —— 開火！"

　　牛虻踉蹌了一下，然後又站穩了。一顆未瞄準的子彈擦傷了他的臉頰，一點點血滴落在他的白領結上。另一顆子彈打中了他膝蓋的上方。火藥的煙霧消散之後，士兵們望過去，看到他仍然微笑着，正用那隻殘廢的手抹去臉上的血。

　　"槍法真差勁，弟兄們！"他説；可憐的士兵們目瞪口呆，牛虻清晰的聲音使他們驚醒了。"再來一次。"

　　……

　　硝煙慢慢散去，飄浮到空中，飄入微明的晨曦之中，他們看見牛虻倒下了，也看到他還活着。一刹那間，官兵們呆呆地站在那裏，好像都變成了石頭，注視着那可怕的東西在地上扭動，掙扎；隨後，醫生和上校都叫了一聲，

rushed forward with a cry, for he had dragged himself up on one knee and was still facing the soldiers, and still laughing.

"Another miss! Try — again, lads — see — if you can't —"

He suddenly swayed and fell over sideways on the grass.

E.L. Voynich: The Gadfly

跑上前去，因為牛虻已經單膝着地，吃力地跪了起來，他仍舊面對着士兵大笑着。

“又沒打中！再——來一次，孩子們——看着——要是你們不能——”

他忽然搖晃起來，側身倒在草地上。

（英）伏尼契：《牛虻》

95　Followed Her Lover[1] to the Tomb

Mathilde followed her lover to the tomb he had chosen for himself. A large number of priests escorted the bier and, alone in her carriage draped in mourning, she bore on her knees, unknown to everyone, the head of the man she had loved so deeply.

Having arrived in this way near the top of one of the towering mountains of the Juras, in the middle of the night, in that little cave magnificently illuminated by countless candles, twenty priests celebrated the Office of the Dead[2]. All the inhabitants of the little mountain villages through which the procession had passed had followed it, drawn by the extraordinary nature of the strange ceremony.

Mathilde appeared in their midst in long mourning garments, and at the end of the service she had several thousand five-franc coins scattered among them.

Henri Beyle Stendhal: The Red and the Black

---

1. her lover：瑪娣爾的情人，即于連。
2. celebrated the Office of the Dead：為死者舉行葬禮，為死者作法事。celebrate：舉行。office：禱告，（宗教）儀式。

九十五　送殯

　　瑪娣爾伴送着她逝去的情人，走向他生前為自己選定的墓地。許多牧師護送着棺架，瑪娣爾身穿喪服獨自坐在送葬的馬車裏，沒有人知道，她的膝上放着她曾深愛的情人的頭顱。

　　半夜時分，一行人到達了珠拉山脈的一個高峯，在接近山頂的小山洞裏，他們點燃了無數蠟燭，場面頗為壯觀，二十個牧師為死者舉行了葬禮。送殯隊伍所經過的小山村的居民們，都被這奇特、古怪的儀式所吸引，紛紛跟隨而來。

　　瑪娣爾身穿長長的喪服站在他們中間，葬禮結束時，她把幾千枚五法郎的硬幣灑向人羣。

（法）斯丹達爾：《紅與黑》

96　The Devil Appears[1]

Then the sick-nurse began to talk and to tell her tales likely to terrify her weak and dying mind. "Some minutes before one dies the Devil appears," she said, "to all. He has a broom in his hand, a saucepan on his head and he utters loud cries. When anybody had seen him, all was over, and that person had only a few moments longer to live"...

Mother Bontemps, who was at last most disturbed in mind, moved about, wrung her hands, and tried to turn her head to look at the other end of the room. Suddenly La Rapet disappeared at the foot of the bed. She took a sheet out of the cupboard and wrapped herself up in it; then she put the iron pot on to her head, so that its three short bent feet rose up like horns, took a broom in her right hand and a tin pail in her left, which she threw up suddenly, so that it might fall to the ground noisily.

Certainly when it came down, it made a terrible noise. Then, climbing on to a chair, the nurse showed herself,

---

1.　拉貝太太負責看護瀕臨死亡的博當大媽，直到她死去，報酬已經講定
　　了。拉貝太太希望病人死得越早越好，便裝神弄鬼，嚇死了老太太。
　　本篇將這個女看護吝嗇、殘忍的嘴臉刻劃得活靈活現。

九十六　裝神弄鬼

　　於是女看護開始講了起來，她給垂死者講了一些恐怖的故事，來刺激她虛弱的神經。"每個人臨死的時候，魔鬼都會出現，"她說，"他手裏拿着一把掃帚，頭上頂着一口鍋，大聲地喊叫。人一見到他就完了，活不了多久了。"……

　　博當大媽終於被嚇壞了，她挪動着身體，雙手絞在一起，想回頭看看房間的另一角。拉貝太太突然消失在牀腳處。她從櫥裏拿出一條被單裏在自己身上，再把鐵鍋扣在頭上，鐵鍋那三隻彎彎的短腳像犄角一樣向上豎起。她右手抓起一把掃帚，左手拿起一隻白鐵桶，猛地向上一拋，好讓它落地時發出響聲。

　　鐵桶掉下來時，確實發出了巨大的聲響。接着，女看

gesticulating and uttering shrill cries into the pot which covered her face, while she menaced the old peasant woman, who was nearly dead, with her broom.

Terrified, with a mad look on her face, the dying woman made a superhuman effort to get up and escape; she even got her shoulders and chest out of bed; then she fell back with a deep sigh.

Guy de Maupassant: "The Devil"

護爬上一把椅子，出現在病人面前，一面手舞足蹈，一面用鐵鍋遮着臉尖聲叫喊，還用掃帚嚇唬那垂死的老農婦。

　　瀕臨死亡的老太太嚇得魂飛魄散，臉上顯出瘋狂的神色，拼命地想爬起來逃走，她甚至把肩膀和胸部都移到了牀外，然後她長嘆了一聲就往後倒下了。

　　　　　　　　　　（法）莫泊桑：《魔鬼》

97   Doing Magic

Miss Watson's[1] nigger, Jim, had a hair-ball[2] as big as your fist, which had been took[3] out of the fourth stomach of an ox, and he used to do magic with it. He said there was a spirit inside of it, and it knowed[4] everything. So I went to him that night and told him pap[5] was here again, for I found his tracks in the snow. What I wanted to know was, what he was going to do, and was he going to stay? Jim got out his hair-ball, and said something over it, and then he held it up and dropped it on the floor. It fell pretty solid, and only rolled about an inch. Jim tried it again, and then another time, and it acted just the same. Jim got down on his knees and put his ear against it and listened. But it warn't[6] no use; he said it wouldn't talk. He said sometimes it wouldn't talk without money. I told him I had an old slick counterfeit quarter...

---

1. Miss Watson：沃森小姐是收養"我"（即小説主人公哈克）的道格拉斯寡婦的妹妹。
2. hair-ball：牛喜愛舔食自身之毛，因此在腸胃中形成毛團。當年美國黑人，常用毛團來占卜。
3. took：應為 taken。哈克未受過良好教育，有時説話不合正規語法。
4. knowed：應為 knew

九十七 占卜

　　沃森小姐的黑奴吉姆有一個拳頭大的毛球，是從一頭牛的第四隻胃裏取出來的，他經常用它施巫術。他說裏面有一個精靈，無所不知。那天晚上我去找他，告訴他爸爸又回來了，我在雪地裏發現了他的蹤迹。我想知道的是，他來幹甚麼，會不會久住？吉姆拿出他的毛球，對它說了些甚麼，然後把它舉起來，一鬆手，毛球落了在地上，落得穩穩的，只滾動了一寸左右。吉姆又試了一次，接着又來了第三次。毛球的滾動同第一次一模一樣。吉姆跪下來，耳朵貼着它聽了聽。但是他說不行，它不肯開口。他說有的時候，不給錢它就不說話。我告訴吉姆，我有一枚表面光滑的兩角五分的舊偽幣。……

---

5. pap：方言，即 papa（爸爸）。哈克的爸爸嗜酒成性，醉酒後常常痛打哈克，他已有一年多未回家。哈克在雪地裏發現了他的腳印，知道爸爸回來了，心裏很不痛快。

6. warn't no use：＝ was no use；warn't 應為 wasn't。

Jim put the quarter under the hair-ball and got down and listened again. This time he said the hair-ball was all right. He said it would tell my whole fortune if I wanted it to. I says[7], go on. So the hair-ball talked to Jim, and Jim told it to me.

Mark Twain: The Adventures of Huckleberry Finn

---

7. I says：應為 "I said"。

吉姆把那枚硬幣放在毛球下面，彎下身子，又聽了聽。這一回他說毛球開口了，如果我願意的話，它可以把我一輩子的命運都告訴我。我說，那就讓它講吧。然後毛球就對吉姆講了起來，吉姆再轉告給我。

　　　（美）馬克・吐溫：《哈克貝利・費恩歷險記》

98 A Charivari

Carol had already seen quite enough of Cy Bogart[1]. On her first evening in Gopher Prairie, Cy had appeared at the head of a "charivari"[2], banging immensely upon a discarded automobile fender. His companions were yelping in imitation of coyotes[3]. Kennicott had felt rather complimented; had gone out and distributed a dollar. But Cy was a capitalist[4] in charivaris. He returned with an entirely new group, and this time there were three automobile fenders and a carnival rattle. When Kennicott again interrupted his shaving, Cy piped, "Naw, you got to give us two dollars," and he got it. A week later Cy rigged a tic-tac[5] to a window of the living-room, and the tattoo out of the darkness frightened Carol into screaming.

Sinclair Lewis: Main Street

---

1. Cy Bogart：一個十四、五歲的紈絝子弟，常搞惡作劇。
2. charivari：喧鬧。此處指敲敲打打地向新郎新娘賀喜。文中 Carol 和 Kennicott 是一對新婚夫婦。
3. coyotes：叢林狼，生活於北美，常於夜晚長嗥。

九十八　惡作劇

對賽·博加特的所作所為，卡蘿爾已經見識夠了。她來戈佛草原鎮的第一晚，賽就帶着一幫人，玩命地敲着一個廢棄的汽車擋泥板，向這對新人"賀喜"。這幫人嗥嗥地學着狼叫。肯尼科特開始還覺得有些受寵若驚，出去送給他們一塊錢。但是賽貪得無厭。不一會兒，他又回來了，帶着一班全新的人馬，這一回他們敲着三個擋泥板，發出狂歡節似的喧鬧。肯尼科特正在刮鬍子，他只好又停下來應付他們。賽尖聲尖氣地説；"這次你得給我們兩塊錢。"他果真得到了兩塊錢。一星期之後，賽又把一個叩窗物安在他們客廳的窗戶上，在深更半夜裏發出的的篤篤的聲音嚇得卡蘿爾尖叫起來。

（美）辛克萊·路易斯：《大街》

---

4. capitalist：意為賽像資本家一樣貪得無厭。

5. tic-tac：指裝在窗或門上的鈕釦類東西，上繫一長綫至遠處，拉動時發出敲擊聲。常為兒童於萬聖節前夕與人開玩笑的遊戲中所用。

99 There Was a Flash

... I heard a cough, then came the chuh-chuh-chuh-chuh[1] — then there was a flash, as when a blast-furnace door is swung open, and a roar that started white and went red and on and on in a rushing wind. I tried to breathe but my breath would not come and I felt myself rush bodily out of myself and out and out and out and all the time bodily in the wind. I went out swiftly, all of myself, and I knew I was dead and that it had all been a mistake to think you just died. Then I floated, and instead of going on I felt myself slide back. I breathed and I was back. The ground was torn up and in front of my head there was a splintered beam of wood.... I tried to move but I could not move. I heard the machine-guns and rifles firing across the river and all along the river.

Ernest Hemingway: A Farewell to Arms

---

1. chuh-chuh-chuh-chuh：擬聲詞，形容炸彈穿過空中時的聲音。

九十九　炸傷

　　……我聽到一種咳嗽似的聲音，然後是嚓、嚓、嚓的
響聲，隨後看到一道閃光，好像一扇鼓風爐的門猛地被打
開了。一陣轟鳴般的響聲傳來，先是帶着白光，接着變成
紅光，一陣疾風似地掃過。我想呼吸，但一口氣也喘不上
來，我感到自己的身體飛出了軀殼，向外飛呀飛，整個身
體一直在風中飛。我的整個人都疾速地飛了出去。我知道
自己死了，又意識到認為自己死去是個錯覺。然後我飄了
起來，但沒有繼續往外飄，我感到身體又滑回軀殼之中。
我喘了口氣，清醒過來。地面被炸得粉碎，我的頭前面是
一片炸碎了的木塊……。我想動一動，但動不了。我聽到
河對面和河邊到處都是機關槍和步槍的響聲。

　　　　　　　　　　（美）海明威：《永別了，武器》

100   They Carried the Wounded In[1]

Outside the post a great many of us lay on the ground in the dark. They carried the wounded in and brought them out. I could see the light come out from the dressing station when the curtain opened and they brought someone in or out. The dead were off to one side. The doctors were working with their sleeves up to their shoulders and were red as butchers. There were not enough stretchers. Some of the wounded were noisy but most were quiet. The wind blew the leaves in the bower over the door of the dressing station and the night was getting cold. Stretcher-bearers came in all the time, put their stretchers down, unloaded them and went away.

Ernest Hemingway: A Farewell to Arms

---

1. 此選段是第一次世界大戰中在意大利前綫搶救傷員的一個場景。

一百　搶救站

　　我們很多傷員都躺在搶救站外面的地上，天色已黑。
他們把傷者抬進抬出。繃紮所的簾子打開了，我看到裏面
的燈光，有人被送進，有人被送出，死者被放在一邊。醫
生們忙碌着，他們的袖子捲得高高的，身上到處是血，就
像屠夫一樣。擔架不夠。有些傷員呻吟着，大多數人則一
聲不吭。繃紮所門上遮蔭的樹葉在風中沙沙作響，夜色中
寒氣襲來。擔架手們不停地走進來，放下擔架，卸下傷
員，然後匆匆離去。

　　　　　　　　　　　(美) 海明威：《永別了，武器》

外國名著行爲描寫一百段 = 100 sketches of
human behaviour from great novels ／ 郭麗
選譯. -- 臺灣初版. -- 臺北市：臺灣商務，
1997 [民86]
　　面；　公分. -- (一百叢書；20)
ISBN 957-05-1363-2 (平裝)

813.6　　　　　　　　　　　85013132

一百叢書 ⑳

外國名著行爲描寫一百段

100 SKETCHES OF HUMAN BEHAVIOUR

FROM GREAT NOVELS

定價新臺幣 300 元

選　譯　者　郭　　麗
主　編　者　張　信　威
　責任編輯　金　　堅
出　版　者　臺灣商務印書館股份有限公司
印　刷　所
　　　　　　臺北市重慶南路 1 段 37 號
　　　　　　電話：(02) 23116118・23115538
　　　　　　傳眞：(02) 23710274
　　　　　　郵政劃撥：0000165-1 號
　　　　　　出版事業
　　　　　　登 記 證：局版北市業字第 993 號

• 1996 年 9 月香港初版
• 1997 年 2 月臺灣初版第一次印刷
• 1999 年 3 月臺灣初版第二次印刷

本書經商務印書館(香港)有限公司授權出版

ISBN　957-05-1363-2（平裝）　　　b 26242000

一百叢書　100 SERIES

英漢・漢英對照

讀者回函卡

感謝您對本館的支持，為加強對您的服務，請填妥此卡，免付郵資寄回，可隨時收到本館最新出版訊息，及享受各種優惠。

姓名：＿＿＿＿＿＿＿＿＿＿＿＿＿＿ 性別：□男 □女

出生日期：＿＿＿年＿＿＿月＿＿＿日

職業：□學生 □公務（含軍警） □家管 □服務 □金融 □製造
　　　□資訊 □大眾傳播 □自由業 □農漁牧 □退休 □其他

學歷：□高中以下（含高中） □大專 □研究所（含以上）

地址：□□□＿＿＿＿＿＿＿＿＿＿＿＿＿＿＿＿＿＿＿＿＿
＿＿＿＿＿＿＿＿＿＿＿＿＿＿＿＿＿＿＿＿＿＿＿＿＿

電話：（H）＿＿＿＿＿＿＿＿＿＿（O）＿＿＿＿＿＿＿＿＿

購買書名：＿＿＿＿＿＿＿＿＿＿＿＿＿＿＿＿＿＿＿＿＿＿

您從何處得知本書？
　　　□書店 □報紙廣告 □報紙專欄 □雜誌廣告 □DM廣告
　　　□傳單 □親友介紹 □電視廣播 □其他

您對本書的意見？（A/滿意 B/尚可 C/需改進）
　　　內容＿＿＿＿ 編輯＿＿＿＿ 校對＿＿＿＿ 翻譯＿＿＿＿
　　　封面設計＿＿＿＿ 價格＿＿＿＿ 其他＿＿＿＿＿＿＿＿

您的建議：＿＿＿＿＿＿＿＿＿＿＿＿＿＿＿＿＿＿＿＿＿＿
＿＿＿＿＿＿＿＿＿＿＿＿＿＿＿＿＿＿＿＿＿＿＿＿＿＿＿
＿＿＿＿＿＿＿＿＿＿＿＿＿＿＿＿＿＿＿＿＿＿＿＿＿＿＿

臺灣商務印書館

台北市重慶南路一段三十七號 電話：（02）23116118・23115538
讀者服務專線：080056196 傳真：（02）23710274
郵撥：0000165-1號 E-mail：cptw@ms12.hinet.net

廣 告 回 信

台灣北區郵政管理局登記證

第 6 5 4 0 號

100臺北市重慶南路一段37號

臺灣商務印書館 收

對摺寄回，謝謝！

傳統現代　並翼而翔

Flying with the wings of tradition and modernity.